Ask Amy Green

LOVE AND OTHER
DRAMA-RAMAS!

Ask Amy Green

LOVE AND OTHER DRAMA-RAMAS!

SARAH WEBB

CANDLEWICK PRESS

Copyright © 2011 by Sarah Webb

All rights reserved. No part of this book may be reproduced, transmitted, or stored in an information retrieval system in any form or by any means, graphic, electronic, or mechanical, including photocopying, taping, and recording, without prior written permission from the publisher.

First U.S. paperback edition 2013

The Library of Congress has cataloged the hardcover edition as follows:

Webb, Sarah.
Ask Amy Green : love and other drama-ramas! / Sarah Webb. — 1st U.S. ed.
p. cm. — (Amy Green)
Summary: Thirteen-year-old Amy Green finds herself surrounded by the drama of romance as her mother prepares for her wedding while working with a handsome celebrity on his biography, Aunt Clover dates a singer, and Mills falls for new student Bailey.
ISBN 978-0-7636-5582-2 (hardcover)
[1. Advice columns — Fiction. 2. Dating (Social customs) — Fiction. 3. Friendship — Fiction. 4. Aunts — Fiction. 5. Ireland — Fiction.]
I. Title. II. Title: Love and other drama-ramas!
PZ7.W3838Asl 2012
[Fic]—dc23   2011048115

ISBN 978-0-7636-5689-8 (paperback)

13 14 15 16 17 18 BVG 10 9 8 7 6 5 4 3 2 1

Printed in Berryville, VA, U.S.A.

This book was typeset in ITC Giovanni.

Candlewick Press
99 Dover Street
Somerville, Massachusetts 02144

visit us at www.candlewick.com

This book is dedicated to Annalie Grainger,
my friend in books.

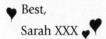

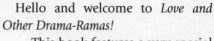

Hello and welcome to *Love and Other Drama-Ramas!*

This book features a very special boy — Bailey Otis. Readers often ask me whether any of the "Ask Amy Green" characters are based on real people, and in Bailey's case the answer is yes. When I was thirteen, a dark-haired boy used to follow me home from school. He never said a word, just walked a few steps behind me — which was a little unnerving.

One day I'd had enough of this creepy behavior, so I spun around and asked him what he was playing at. He shrugged and said that I looked nice and he just wanted to talk to me. Then he gave me this lovely shy smile from under his floppy fringe.

So we talked.

It turned out we had a lot in common — we were both big readers and loved old movies — and we quickly became friends. He told me his mum had died recently, and he was having a tough time dealing with it. A few months after we first spoke, he and his dad moved away and we lost contact, but I've always wondered what happened to him. I hope he's happy.

Bailey Otis was inspired by my lost friend. I hope you enjoy Amy, Clover, and Bailey's story.

Best,

Sarah XXX

It matters not how strait the gate,
How charged with punishments the scroll.
I am the master of my fate:
I am the captain of my soul.

From "Invictus" by William Ernest Henley

♥ Chapter 1

"Adults are crazy," I moan to my best friend, Mills, as we trudge through mounds of soggy autumn leaves, sending a musty smell into the air, on our way to school. "Dave's convinced Mum's going to elope with the Irish Surfing Chef. He's completely delusional." (Dave is Mum's much-put-upon fiancé.)

Mills's eyes widen, and she gives a little shiver. "You mean Finn Hunter? Holy moly, Amy, I'd elope with him! He's gorgeous. Those smoldering green eyes. Those abs." She pauses and looks at me. "Did Dave catch your mum kissing the telly while Finn was on?"

I smile. "Nope, she's only ghostwriting Finn's book for him — which means they'll be working up close and *personal*. That's why Dave is so worried."

"Ghostwriting?" She frowns. "Your mum and Finn Hunter are writing a horror story together? Haunted houses, vampires, that sort of thing?"

I laugh. "Nothing to do with spooks or werewolves or ax-wielding maniacs. Mum's going to help him write *his* book. Finn will tell her what he'd like in the book — characters, plot, that kind of stuff — she'll make notes and then write it for him. All the stars have ghostwriters, apparently — Katie Price, Madonna. Sounds pretty lazy, if you ask me, but if it pulls Mum out of the Mama Doldrums, then hallelujah."

"Is she still in one of her funny moods?" (Mills knows Mum only too well.)

"Yep. Gothic glum for days now. Anyone would think she'd morphed into Bella Swan. But working with Finn is bound to cheer her up. She'll be spending hours and hours with him, and some of the meetings will be in our house." I wiggle my eyebrows at Mills. "Imagine — just the two of them, huddled over Mum's laptop."

Mills squeals. She jumps up and down on the spot and clutches my arm. "Can I meet him, Ames?" she begs. "Please, please, *pleeeease*?"

"Of course. But keep it to yourself. No one's supposed to know that Finn has a ghostwriter. I wish

we could tell the D4s, though. They'd be so envious."
(The D4s are the mean girls at our school, Saint John's.)

"It's a shame, all right. But forget the D4s — I want details, girl, details. What's Finn like in real life? And if the book's not a gory bloodfest, is it one of those swoony romance novels my mum reads? The ones with gorgeous millionaires and champagne and, you know, kissing and stuff?" Mills's face goes a little pink.

I laugh. "Not exactly."

And I tell her the whole story. . . .

♥ Chapter 2

It all started yesterday late afternoon, when Mum made a rather startling announcement in the kitchen. "Remember the book I was hired to ghostwrite?" she said, looking at me and Dave smugly. (Mum's a television scriptwriter, but she hasn't worked since my baby sister, Evie, was born eight months ago.) "Well, I have news," she continued, ignoring Evie, who was squirming in her high chair and throwing mushed-up food around as usual. "I'm starting work on it next week. Would you like to know the title?"

"The suspense is killing me," I said with a bored sigh.

"Less of the Miss Snark, Amy Green," Mum said. "The book — my very first proper published novel —

is called *Hot Love.*" Her eyes were glistening. She was clearly very excited about the whole thing.

Dave grinned at her. "*Hot Love?* Bring it on, Sylvie." He gave a saucy wink.

I scrunched up my nose. "*Eeeuw,* please. I'm only thirteen, people. Remember?"

"Amy's right, Dave!" Mum flicked a tea towel at him, hitting him on the head. "There are quite enough children in this house already, thank you very much." She tightened the belt of her waffle-cotton bathrobe, which she was wearing over her smart black trousers and white shirt. It looked pretty odd.

"What's it about, then, Mum?" I asked, hoping to change the subject. (My parental types can be so embarrassing sometimes.)

"I'm not sure exactly. The line was pretty bad, and I couldn't really hear what Britta — she's the celebrity's agent — was saying. But from the title, I guess it's chick lit. Maybe set in the Caribbean or something. Lots of sun, and hunky men and bed-hopping."

"Mum!" I could feel my face reddening.

Dave smiled. "Sex is a part of life, Amy. Better get used to it." He started to sing "Circle of Life" from *The Lion King.*

I cringed. They're both mortifying. Don't they get

it — I don't want to talk about hot love, bed-hopping, or S-E-X with grown-up-ians. Not now, not ever.

"In fact, Britta will be here soon," Mum said. "I hope you'll keep Evie and Alex well away from the living room, Dave. It's an important meeting."

I stared at her. It's official: adults are certifiably crazy. Why would you hold an important meeting in *our* living room? It's full of Thomas the Tank Engine toys and smells of Evie's poopy nappies.

"Why didn't you suggest somewhere glam like a posh hotel or something, Mum?" I asked. "The living room's a state."

"Britta said it was easier to meet here since she was in the area anyway. She's bringing her celebrity client with her."

Dave was also staring at her. "Hang on a sec. That meeting is *now*? I have to cover for someone at work today. I told you that earlier."

"Dave! You absolutely did not."

Dave ran his hand over his shorn head. "I did. You must have forgotten. Your brain's like mush these days."

"How dare you? And what on earth am I going to do now? Britta will be here any second. I can't have Alex running around my feet; it'll look so unprofessional." (She had a point — Alex is a toddler terrorist.)

Dave and Mum's eyes swiveled in my direction at exactly the same time.

I screwed up my face. "Please, no. Not the babies. Anything but the babies." I was only half joking.

Dave put his hand in the back pocket of his jeans and pulled out a crumpled ten-euro note. "Please, Amy," he begged.

"Fine. As usual I'm just the resident house elf at Fifteen Sycamore Park. But if Alex bites me again, I'm biting back."

To be honest, I wasn't all that bothered. Anything's better than homework—even babysitting—and if it saved Dave's bacon, I was happy to help. After a rather shaky start, I've started to really like Dave. He's kind and he cares about Mum and the babies, and me, I guess—more than he cares about himself sometimes, I think.

He and Mum are getting married on New Year's Eve, if they ever get around to organizing it, that is. Dave used to be a musician, but now he's a nurse at Saint Vincent's Hospital, and his work shifts are all over the place, so he gets very little time at home. Mum never stops moaning about it and the fact that when he is at home, he spends all his time on his Dinoduck songs. He's hoping to be the next big thing in toddler rock. It'll never, ever happen, though.

Trust me, I've heard the songs. And since Mum is so busy with the babies, the wedding plans are moving very slowly. At least the bachelorette party is sorted out — my crazy seventeen-year-old aunt Clover, me, and Monique, Mum's best friend, are planning that!

"Better get going," Dave said. He held Mum's head and kissed her on both cheeks. "Best of luck with Britta and her star. I'm dying to hear who it is. Chin up, and remember to smile."

Mum just nodded, her lower lip wobbling as she watched Dave leave. I think she was wishing she could go with him. (She can be a bit emotionally fragile sometimes.)

Evie swung her spoon while Mum was distracted, and a lump of puréed apple caught Mum's shoulder and then splattered to the floor. Ah, the bathrobe did have a point!

"Are you sure you're going to be all right with the babies, Amy?" Mum asked, wiping the splodge away with some damp paper towels. "Maybe I should ask Gramps or Clover to help."

Clover — now there was an idea. I hadn't seen her for days, and I was starting to have withdrawal symptoms. Life's always much more fun with Clover around to shake, rattle, and roll things up. Besides, we had stuff to talk about—Mum's fab bachelorette party for one!

After settling Evie on a rug in the backyard and handing Alex his favorite fire engine, I threw Clover a quick text.

The doorbell rang, and I peered in through the kitchen window. Mum was scrabbling to untie her bathrobe and brushing her hair off her face with her hands, all seemingly at the same time—and she was practically hyperventilating.

"I'll get it, Mum," I said, coming back inside. I figured she needed a few minutes to gather her wits (what she had left of them).

She smiled gratefully. "Thanks, Amy. That must be Britta. Show her into the living room, will you? I'll be there in a second." She took several deep breaths and wiped her palms on the front of her trousers.

I walked into the hall and swung the front door open, expecting to see a woman standing there. But instead, it was Finn Hunter, the Irish Surfing Chef from the telly! What on earth was he doing on our doorstep? I could feel my blood thumping in my chest, and I couldn't say a thing, I just froze, gawking at him.

"Hiya," he said, giving me a warm smile. His

silver thumb ring winked in the light as he pushed his sun-bleached fringe out of his green eyes. He had a distinctive face, long and angular, with a nutty-brown surfer's tan. In fact, his features were so loaded with sharp edges, you could cut yourself on them. He shouldn't be good-looking but, boy, is he!

"I'm here to see Sylvie," he said, which was just as well since I was still standing in dumbfounded silence and the atmosphere was starting to feel a little uncomfortable. "I'm Finn. Finn Hunter. I'm here about the book. Britta sent me. Can I come in?"

Holy moly, as Mills would say. Finn Hunter was Mum's celebrity. She was going to freak out. The Irish Surfing Chef!

"Sorry, yes, of course." I stood back.

As he brushed past me, I got a waft of old leather and the sea. He was wearing a beaten-up brown leather jacket and an old Guns n' Roses T-shirt over baggy combat shorts and black flip-flops. Cuter and cuter.

"Mum, your guest is here," I shouted into the kitchen, and then showed him into the living room, kicking Alex's wooden train set under the sofa as I went. "Sorry about the mess."

He gave a laugh. "No worries. You should see my place."

Mum walked in the door straightening her shirt.

She stopped dead and stared when she saw Finn, her jaw dropping caveman low.

"Ugghhh," she managed eventually, adding to the caveman impression. Her face had gone Barbie pink.

Mum's mad about Finn Hunter. She thinks he's much hotter than Jamie Oliver, and that's saying a lot. I bet Mum never expected him to turn up in her living room!

"*You're* the . . . celebrity?" she said, spluttering only slightly.

Finn smiled. "You know who I am, then?"

Mum nodded wordlessly.

"And you're Sylvie, right?"

She nodded again.

"Britta sends her apologies," he went on. "Had to fly out to Portugal at the last minute to rescue one of her clients. Said to go ahead without her. To talk about the book and stuff."

Mum's eyes goggled. "I'm going to be ghostwriting *your* book?"

He shrugged. "I guess. If you'll have me."

"Of course I'll have you." And Mum's face colored even deeper. She shook her head and giggled. "I'm sorry. It's just so weird seeing you in the flesh. And close enough to touch. Not that I would, of course." She colored still more.

"Cool," Finn said, grinning at her. "In that case, welcome to Team Hunter. I've heard great things about you from Britta. You used to write for *Fair City*, yeah?"

"Senior scriptwriter," Mum said proudly. "I've been trying to get a book published for years. This is a really exciting opportunity for me. Have you started plotting it out yet?"

"I tried bashing out a few pages, but I didn't have much luck. It was all over the place. I'm dyslexic, you see, and I can only type with two fingers. That's why Britta suggested getting professional help."

"Dyslexic?" I piped up with interest. (Seth, my boyfriend, is dyslexic. He *hates* showing anyone his handwriting, and he's pretty sensitive about his spelling too.)

"Yeah," Finn said. "Failed all my school exams. Could barely string a sentence together on paper. And we had no special teachers or anything like that in my day. They just thought I was thick. I spent nearly every afternoon in detention for giving cheek in class, but I only talked back 'cause I was so frustrated. The school pretty much wrote me off. Pack of kooks." He broke off. "Sorry, it still gets to me. Look, that's one of the reasons I want to do this book — to show kids you don't have to ace your exams to be successful.

You can do anything if you set your mind to it and work hard. The most important thing is to find your passion in life. The thing that makes life spark for you, you know? Mine's cooking." He grinned and ran his hands through his hair. "Sorry, end of lecture. Oh, and Britta says the book will be good for my profile — all the other celebrity chefs have memoirs."

"Finn, did you just say *memoir*?" Mum asked quietly.

"Sure. I'm a chef. I'd hardly be trying to write the next great Irish novel. The publishers want to throw in some nonsense about my food philosophy. I don't really have one, other than using fresh ingredients, so you can just make that bit up. You're used to inventing things, Sylvie, right? And we can throw in a few of my fave recipes for good measure. Britta suggested calling it *Pot Luck: The Finn Hunter Story*. What do you think?"

"*Pot Luck*?" Mum whispered to herself, her face pale.

"You OK, Mum?" I asked.

She nodded, although she looked flabbergasted — so much for her being the next Marian Keyes or Cecelia Ahern. And she hates cooking. She's always complaining about having to cook for us every night. The problem is I happen to know she's in debt and already counting on the book money to pay for some of the wedding expenses. Oops. It looked like Mum was in serious trouble.

"Do you like cooking, Sylvie?" Finn asked her.

I tried to think sad "pet dying" thoughts to stop myself from laughing hysterically.

Mum looked at Finn for a moment, as though considering his question. "I used to. Before I had children. These days my favorite kind of food is food cooked by somebody else."

Finn gave a deep chuckle. "I hear you. Me too."

The doorbell rang again, so I excused myself to answer it. I was hoping it was Clover — she'd die when she saw Finn. I swung open the door and grinned. My wish had been granted.

"Clover, you'll never guess who's sitting on our sofa," I hissed before she'd even had a chance to step inside the door. "Only the Irish Surfing Chef!"

Clover gasped. "What? No way, dude. That's awesome," she said, imitating his accent. (Although Finn's originally from Northern Ireland, on his show he sometimes sounds more like an Aussie surfer than an Irish guy.) "What's *he* doing here?"

"Remember that novel Mum thought she was writing, *Hot Love*? It's actually his memoir. *Pot Luck.*"

Clover winced. "Poor Sylvie. She must be

crushed — she thought this was going to be her big break. But she's got to be psyched about spending time with Finn. I wonder what Dave will make of it. He's not exactly a Finn Hunter fan. Tell me, is Mr. Awesome as showstopping in the flesh?"

I grinned. "Affirmative. I think Mum's still in shock."

Clover crossed herself. "Bless me, Beanie, I'm going in. Watch my back in case I faint."

And with that, she bounded into the living room. She stopped dead in front of Finn to gawk at him. "Amy's right," she said. "You're stunning in real life."

My cheeks danced with embarrassment. "Clover!"

Luckily Alex started yelling ultra loudly. Saved by the baby!

"I'll get him, Mum," I said, "and leave you guys to talk business. Come on, Clover."

"Thanks, Amy." Mum cleared her throat and glared at Clover, who wasn't budging. Clover's eyes were glued to Finn's cheekbones, so I grabbed her arm and pulled. She was still tinkling her fingers at him as I yanked her out the door. "Bye, Finn," she said. "It was epic meeting you. Back to the groms now."

I closed the door firmly behind her. "Groms?" I asked her.

"Grommets. Little baby surfers. You need to

watch Finn's show more, Beanie. And did you check out that face? Smokin'." She licked her finger, pressed it against my arm, and made a sizzling noise. "Pity he's such an oldie. He's at least twenty-seven. But I wonder if Saffy would go for a *Goss* piece on cute Irish teen surfers. What do you think, teen journo guru?"

Clover's the agony aunt for a teen magazine called the *Goss*, and I help her solve all the readers' problem letters. Clover also writes features and sometimes gets to interview Hollywood movie stars, like Matt Munroe and Efa Valentine, which is *très* cool. Clover was starting college the following week, so I wasn't sure what was going to happen. Sometimes I daydream about taking over for her and calling the problem page "Ask Amy Green," with a pic of me at the top and my own special logo — but I know that's not going to happen. Saffy, Clover's editor, is hardly going to employ a thirteen-year-old. So for the moment I'm just Clover's helper — which is still a lot of fun!

Alex appeared at the top of the stairs — I'd forgotten all about him! He was naked from the waist down and swinging his nappy over his head like a cowboy lasso. His face was streaked with greasy red marks that looked suspiciously like Mum's new crimson Chanel lipstick. (When Mum's in the moody blues, she always buys expensive lipstick — it's one of her many weaknesses.)

"What are you doing up there, young man?" I asked him. "You're supposed to be outside."

He just giggled and looked delighted with himself.

"Alex, you're a right mess," Clover said. "Sticky babies? That's my cue to leave. I have surfers to track down, you know. Tell Finn I said *slán*."

"Clover, you can't just skip off and leave me to —" But she was already out the door.

And as I told Mills on the way to school, breakfast this morning was — how can I put this — interesting. Mum seemed to have gotten over the shock of writing Finn's memoir and was launching herself into the whole project with gusto. But as Clover predicted, Dave was in a right huff.

"Ten meetings with the man?" he grumbled. "I don't see why he can't use a Dictaphone and send you the tapes."

Mum sighed. "As I keep telling you, it's going to be a collaboration. I'll need Finn to help me understand the motivation behind his actions. We planned it all out at our meeting yesterday, and we both agreed the text needs to capture his own distinctive voice." She smiled a little dreamily. "Finn has already told me the bones of his story. He's got quite a past. He grew up in County Antrim, and his dad died in a fishing accident when he was eleven. After that he went off the rails for a few years. He caused a lot of trouble in school and ended up dropping out at fifteen to work in a kitchen as a dishwasher. At seventeen he ran away to London, got a job at the River Café, and the rest is history. He's made a lot of mistakes in his life, but he's trying to make amends. He does a load of work for that Irish charity, Unity — he's been over to Haiti and everything. I think he's awesome."

Awesome? I tried not to laugh. Mum was obviously already under Finn Hunter's spell.

"That's all very well, but I won't have him muscling in and causing problems." Dave was still scowling like a sulky toddler.

Mum looked confused. "Problems? What are you on about, Dave?" She stared at him for a second and then started to smile. "I get it. You're jealous. You think I'm going to run off into the sunset with the man, don't you?"

"No!" But from the intent way that Dave was staring at the toast crumbs on his plate, I reckoned Mum had cracked it.

"I wish," Mum said. "Once you meet Finn, you'll realize how ludicrous you're being. Tell him, Amy."

"She's right," I said. "He's way too young and cool for Mum."

Mum harrumphed. "Thanks a lot, Amy."

Jeepers, I couldn't win. I was only trying to help.

"For the record, I'm still not keen on the whole project." Dave stood up, clattered his plate into the sink, and marched out the door.

I sighed. More family drama-rama. Mum had opened her mouth to say something, so I grabbed my schoolbag and scuttled out, too, before she had the chance.

I ran toward the mailbox to meet Mills and poured out the whole story.

♥ Chapter 3

After all the excitement of the morning, everything's yawningly normal at school until lunch break, when Loopy (real name Miss Lupin) bounces down the hall in her usual uniform of Birkenstocks, tie-dyed skirt, and Fair Trade T-shirt. She sweeps past me and Mills in a waft of patchouli. For some reason, Annabelle Hamilton and the rest of the D4s are trailing after her: orange rats to her eco Pied Piper. Good to see their fake-tan addiction is still intact—the day they break that habit, the shopkeepers of Ireland will suffer drastically.

"What's going on?" I ask Mills.

She looks sheepish. "Oops. I forgot to tell you. It was the talk of French class. Miss Stringer has resigned from the drama club 'cause of her teeth."

"Her teeth?"

"Hard-core train tracks. Top and bottom. Apparently, she can barely talk properly, let alone produce a musical. She's so self-conscious, she won't open her mouth."

I shake my head and tut. "First the olds steal our Gaga, then our *Glee,* and now our dentistry! It's not right, my friend. And isn't Stringer a bit long in the tooth for extreme orthodontics?" I grin at my own bad joke.

Mills groans. "That's terrible, Amy! But you'd think, wouldn't you? However, as we both know, olds can be mighty strange! Anyway, Miss Lupin's taken over the drama club. She doesn't have time to direct a musical, though, 'cause of all her other commitments, so she's come up with a compromise until Miss Stringer's feeling up to returning."

"Which is?"

Mills nods at Loopy, who is now standing in front of the school notice board, a sheet of paper clutched against her chest. The D4s are surging toward her like a pack of rabid football fans. "She said she'd announce it at lunch break. Hence the D4 scrum."

The air smells of D4 ambition—they are all wannabe celebrities.

Loopy yelps as one of them stands on her toe.

"For heaven's sake, move back, girls," she says. "I'm not putting this up until you give me some space."

"Everyone, like, back," Annabelle, D4 Queen Bee, commands in her recently acquired quasi-Californian accent. (For some reason, Annabelle thinks it's cool to sound like a *90210* extra instead of a bog-standard Dublin girl.) Her minions shuffle back reluctantly in their navy docksiders.

Loopy pins the notice up, and Annabelle immediately shrieks, "There's going to be a Saint John's talent contest on Halloween. The J Factor. Auditions start next week. I'm so going to win!" She beams, showing off her perfect teeth, and begins dancing along the corridor, pumping her arms in the air and rapping, "Who's got the J Factor? I've got the J Factor. Who's gonna beat me? No one's gonna beat me."

"Are you entering?" I ask Mills quietly. "You're brilliant at piano."

She smiles gently. "I don't think classical music's quite what they're after, Ames, but thanks." She links arms with me. "Come on, let's find the boys."

We walk outside to where Seth and Bailey are standing by the wall, waiting for us. Bailey Otis is new this year, but he and Seth are already as thick as thieves. My heart gives its familiar lurch at the sight of Seth. Even though we've been together for nearly four months now, his sky-blue eyes and blond floppy hair still make my heart beat faster.

And Mills is as crazy about Mr. OMG Otis. I don't blame her — he is tongue-hanging-out cute. Piercing emerald eyes, jet-black shaggy hair, cheekbones to die for. They've officially been boyfriend/girlfriend for three weeks now, and most of the time you need a crowbar to separate them.

"Hey, Amy." Seth kisses me gently, his lips warm and firm against mine. I blush a little, hoping none of the D4s have spotted us. They have a nasty habit of calling "Get a room" at anyone apart from a fellow D4 showing any PDA (public display of affection) at school.

"Field hockey steps?" he says. (It's where we always have lunch unless it's raining.)

I nod. "May as well make the most of the sun. Nice penguin, by the way." I smile and nudge him playfully with my shoulder. There's a cartoon drawing of a penguin with a heart on its tummy on the brown-paper sandwich bag he's clutching. Polly, Seth's mum, is always drawing on his lunch. Sweet!

He grins and rolls his eyes. "Polly's a nightmare." But I know he doesn't mean it. There's only the two of them, and they're very close. She had breast cancer recently, but she's having treatment in the hospital Dave works at and is doing really well now, thankfully.

I go to say hi to Bailey, but it's too late—he and Mills are already smooching. Bailey's large DJ headphones are still clamped over his ears, though, like two halves of a coconut.

"See you at the steps, lovebirds," I call.

"Remember to keep that tongue in time with the tunes, Otis," Seth adds.

Bailey doesn't stop kissing Mills, but he does lift one finger in a rather rude gesture and waggles it at us.

Seth laughs heartily. "Surprised you can hear me, mate."

At the steps we sit down and start eating. By the time Mills and Bailey reach us—his arm slung around her shoulders, her fingers entwined in one of his belt loops—we've almost finished. Bailey sits on the top step and Mills arranges herself on the second, so she can rest her head against his chest. She swivels around, and they start snogging again.

"Please!" I say. "I'm trying to eat, people."

They break away, and Mills giggles, her cheeks flushed. "Sorry."

"Apologies, Greenster," Bailey says with a grin. "Just can't help myself." He starts singing an old tune that Dave sometimes plays called "Addicted to Love," changing the lyrics from "Might as well face it, I'm addicted to love" to "Might as well face it, I'm addicted to Mills." He's got an amazing voice, deep and husky, yet caramel smooth. As he serenades her, Mills gazes at him dreamily.

And moments later, they're kissing again.

Seth stands up and holds out his hand to me. "I think we should just leave them to it. They clearly have things to discuss. Telepathically."

I grin. "*Tongue*-apathically, you mean?"

♥ Chapter 4

Mills rests her back against the lockers during break on Wednesday and smiles at me. "Fancy a trip to Dundrum after school to mooch around the shops and grab some food? Come on, Ames, it'll be fun."

I think about it for a second. We haven't gone shopping, just the two of us, for ages. I have enough babysitting money stashed in my wallet to pay for some eats, and so long as Mum doesn't mind, why not? It would be nice to spend some time with Mills, alone. I'm happy for her, honestly I am — Bailey's great — but I do miss *us*.

I smile back at her. "I was going to hang out with Seth, but he won't mind. Girls' day out, yeah! Like you say, it'll be fun."

A shadow crosses Mills's face. "I thought the boys could come too. You know, a double date."

I make a pained noise. "A double date? Mills, are you deranged? Seth would rather die than go on a *double date*. Was this Bailey's idea? Is Bailey-wailey dying to go on a *double date*?" Mills and her whole Otis obsession is bringing out the worst in me.

Her face flares up. "Why are you being so mean, Amy? And don't say anything to Bailey. It was my idea, OK? I just thought it would be nice to spend some time together, the four of us." She looks genuinely upset, which makes me feel a bit guilty.

"I suppose it could be all right," I say slowly.

She brightens. "Do you think Seth would be up for it?"

"I'll ask him."

"Thanks, Ames. And I promise I'll never utter the words 'double date' again as long as I live." She crosses her heart with her finger. "Or couples' day."

I shake my head and sigh. "I'll pretend I didn't hear that one."

"So how's the double date going for you so far?" I whisper on the rare occasion Mills is not clinging to Bailey's arm like a limpet.

"Shush," she hisses, looking around frantically. "He might hear you."

We're in Music City, and the boys are poring over the CD racks, checking out the latest releases. I'd much rather be in Zara or H&M checking out *their* latest releases, but Mills insisted. "We love Music City, don't we, Ames?" she said when Bailey suggested it, and gave me a loaded look.

"Certainly do," I agreed. "Can't wait to rummage through the rails. I mean, racks." Seth gave me a funny look but didn't say anything.

Bailey and Seth have moved toward the listening posts and clamped two sets of headphones over their ears, so I take the opportunity to talk to Mills properly. "Why are you pretending you hate clothes shopping?" I ask her. "Seth is baffled. The last time he came to Dundrum with us, you spent two hours trying on dresses in Zara."

She clutches my arm. "Amy, keep your voice down."

I roll my eyes and point at Bailey, who is nodding his head in time to the music, eyes shut and a look of concentration on his face. "He's so engrossed in his tunes, a herd of elephants could stampede in here and he wouldn't notice. But, Mills, seriously, you have to stop trying to be someone you're not."

Her eyes go all wide and scared. "But if he finds out what I'm really like, he'll break up with me."

"What? That you like shopping? Mills, Bailey's not that fickle, surely. And if he is, then he doesn't deserve you."

Mills fiddles with the old leather waistcoat of Dave's that she's borrowed off me. (It's her new "rock chick" look and is designed to impress Bailey.) "That's OK for you to say. You're not going out with the cutest boy in school."

I stare at her. "Hello? Seth's no slacker in the looks department."

"Sorry, I know. But you don't understand the pressure." She gives another breathy sigh.

OK, now my skin is starting to prickle with irritation. Before I have a chance to say anything, though, she continues, "Do you think the boys would prefer pizza or burgers?"

"What do *you* want to eat, Mills?"

"I'm easy. I'll let the boys decide."

"Amelia Starr," I say sternly, "our great-great-grandmothers did not chain themselves to railings or burn their bras so that you could be such a girlie marshmallow. *You* make a decision. Pizza or burgers?"

She hesitates, her eyes big and startled like a deer

caught in headlights. "Um . . . um . . . pizza," she stammers. "No . . . no . . . burgers."

"I'll accept your first answer. Pizza it is."

"But what if Bailey—"

I cut her off. "Then he'll have to put up with it."

"Who'll have to put up with it?" Seth asks, appearing beside us. Bailey is nowhere to be seen.

"Nothing," Mills says quickly.

"Fancy a pizza?" I ask him.

He smiles and nods easily. "Sure. Bailey was just saying he'd kill for a pepperoni special."

I smile at Mills smugly, but she's distracted. "Where's Bailey?" she asks Seth, looking panicked. "He hasn't gone home, has he?"

"Patience, Grasshopper," Seth says, giving me a wink. He knows it's one of my expressions. I stole it from Clover.

A few seconds later, Bailey reappears swinging a small Music City bag on his index finger. He hands it to Mills. "Present," he says simply.

Mills's face lights up like a Christmas tree. "For me?" She pulls a CD out of the bag. "The new *Glee*. Thanks, Bailey." Her face drops. "But you hate *Glee*. You say they murder perfectly good songs."

He shrugs. "Yeah. But I know you dig that happy-clappy musicals stuff. I've checked out your iPod."

He gives her a wide smile. "You can run, Mills, but you can't hide."

Mills's cheeks go scarlet. "I like other stuff too," she mumbles. "Like the Golden Lions and, um, the Red Hot Chili People."

Bailey grins and throws his arm over her shoulders. "Now, did I hear someone say pizza? Come on, my little cheerleader," he tells her in a mock American accent. "You can torture me with some cheesy *Glee* songs on the way."

A Piece of Rome is hopping, but we manage to get a small table in the corner. Once we've ordered, Seth leans in to me. "Sorry I don't have the moolah to get you anything," he says.

"That's OK," I say, and then noticing that Mills and Bailey are holding hands across the table, I roll my eyes at him.

He smiles. "Rock, paper, scissors, Bailey?" he says, holding out a closed fist.

Bailey looks over at him, his eyes suddenly dark. "What? Now?"

Seth puts his hands up in the air. "Only joking, mate. Just trying to reclaim your digits from Mills the human octopus. You'll need them to eat."

Bailey still doesn't look impressed, but Mills is

smiling. "Not funny, Seth," she says, punching him on the shoulder.

Seth puts his hands around his throat and pretends that a monster is dragging him to the floor.

"Hellupp, hellupp," he squeals. "I'm being eaten by Mills the human octopus."

It's ridiculous but hilarious, and we all start laughing — even, to my relief, Bailey. Everyone is staring at us, but we don't care. I'm laughing so much, tears are rolling down my cheeks, and Bailey is giving big whoopy belly laughs while Mills is trying to look indignant.

"Stop laughing, Bailey," Mills says — but even she's holding her stomach from all the giggling.

Finally Seth stops, and I gulp in deep breaths and try to stop chuckling too.

"You nearly got us all thrown out, man." Bailey grins.

Seth shrugs. "Can't help being such a born comedian."

I groan. "See what I have to put up with? You're delusional, Seth."

"But you love me anyway." He grabs a bread stick, breaks it in half, and sticks the pieces under his top lip. "Marry me, Bella."

I start laughing again. "Seth, stop! I can't take any more. My stomach is killing me."

In the bus on the way home, Mills and I share a seat so the boys can sit together and listen to Bailey's iPod. (He always carries a spare set of headphones in case Mills wants them — barf!) It's strangely sweet seeing the boys bobbing their heads in time to the same song.

I nudge Mills with my shoulder. "Enjoy the double date?"

"I wish every day could be like today. And you?"

"Best day ever." I put my head on her shoulder, and we both sigh blissfully.

♥ Chapter 5

"Oy, Bean Machine, what's up?" Clover appears in the doorway to my bedroom that night. She sits down on my bed and puts her arm around my shoulders.

I shrug it off a tad grumpily. "Nothing."

"Sounds like something to me. Want to talk about it?"

I shake my head wordlessly.

She smiles gently. She seems quieter today, not her usual Tigger-bouncy self. "OK, then. I have something here that might take your mind off whatever's bothering you — the latest *Goss* agony-aunt letters. Want a go?" She pulls a purple folder out of her smart black patent-leather bag (another piece swiped from the *Goss* fashion cupboard, no doubt) and taps it with a finger.

I sigh. "Can't we do it another night? I'm not in the mood for other people's grumblings right now."

"Mood-smood. I have deadlines, Beanie, you know that. You can't weasel out of your agony-aunt duties that easily. But first, tell your old aunt Clover what's up. Pweetty pweese? A problem shared is a problem halved and all that nonsense." She nudges me with her shoulder.

I give her a half-smile (it's all I can manage) and sigh again, so deeply I half expect to blow her across the room like the house of straw in the *Three Little Pigs*. "Oh, it's just Mills," I say glumly.

"What happened? Did you guys have a fight?"

I shake my head. "Nothing like that. It's just that she and Bailey are glued at the hip, and it's driving me crazy. Honestly, they can't keep their paws off each other. It's tragic-o. We had a really nice afternoon. The four of us — me, Mills, Seth, and Bailey — wandered around the shops in Dundrum, had a pizza, and then got the bus back to Dun Laoghaire together. Seth had to get home, so he jumped on a DART, which meant I was left walking with the two of them like a prize lemon. Mills barely said a word to me, and they stopped at every lamppost to have a kiss! It was going to take hours to walk home. In the end I said I was late for babysitting and ran on ahead."

Clover is staring at me, a smile flickering on her lips. "Not jealous are you, Beanie?"

"No! Don't get me wrong. I like Bailey and, let's be frank, he's heaven on legs to look at. Plus he's very decent to Mills — got her a CD today and everything. But I'm still not sure about him. There's something about him that doesn't quite add up. He never talks about his past and clams up if you ask him about his previous school, and he gets really moody for no reason. Sometimes I think he's hiding something."

"Oooh, I do love a boy with a big, dark secret. I wonder what it could be." Clover grins, then stops when she sees that I'm not smiling. "This is seriously getting to you, isn't it, Bean Machine?"

"I guess the truth is I feel a bit abandoned," I admit. "I know it must sound stupid — I mean, I still see her every day in school and everything — but she's changed in the last few weeks. It's all Bailey this and Bailey that. She's obsessed. It's like my best friend has been abducted and replaced by a boy-crazed alien replica. And she's crazy about a boy she barely even knows! I'm her best friend. We've known each other since we were babies."

Clover sighs. "Friendship is hard, Bean Machine. Make no mistake. You should try talking to her. Maybe she's in such a love haze, she can't see or act straight.

It happens — especially to girls like Mills. She does tend to view boys through rose-tinted Romeo-and-Juliet glasses, doesn't she? And it's her first proper Irish *garçon, oui?*"

I nod. "Yes, and maybe she doesn't realize what a ninny she's being. I guess I'll try talking to her and hope that the boy-mad lenses fall from her deluded eyes soon. But I am seriously worried about her. I suppose Bailey could just be very private, but I don't want to see Mills get hurt. I've never seen her so crazy about anyone."

"I guess you have to be her safety net, Beanie: catch her fall if it all goes belly-up. That's what friends are for." Clover smiles at me gently. "Now speaking of problems . . ." She opens the plastic folder, pulls out two pieces of paper, and dangles them in front of my face. "I have some rather interesting ones here that will take your mind off things. *Número uno* involves a friendship dilemma, in fact. Let's start with that one. Because *ze* second — *ooh-la-la! Très, très* tricky, *mon amie*. Read them out loud, Beanie. I need to beautify my toes," she says, pulling a bottle of glittery teal nail polish out of her bag. She draws her legs up and opens the bottle. The acrid smell fills the room.

I scowl at her. "Don't get that on my duvet, Clover. Mum will murder me."

She rolls her eyes. "Yes, Mills."

I give a short laugh. It *is* exactly the kind of thing Mills would say, all right.

I clear my throat and start to read:

Dear Clover and Amy,

The name's Frizzy and I have a big problem. I have three bfs — I'll call them Kylie, Danni, and Cheryl, in case they're reading — and recently they've been acting seriously schizoid.

We haven't been bfs all that long. I used to be bbfs with a girl called Susie, but she's kinda quiet and all she ever wants to do is talk about her drama club (she's pretty good at acting), play Wii, and moon over Jacob from *Twilight*. That's OK some of the time — I'm a bit of a Twerd myself — but not all the time. Still, she listens to me moan about the tiresome trio, I guess, and never complains. She's pretty nice that way.

But K, D, and C are great fun and way more popular in school than Susie. They make me laugh — a lot. They're always cracking jokes about other girls in our class. Yes, sometimes they make fun of me, calling me ginger rasta girl — my hair is orange and can go a bit frizzy sometimes — but they tease everyone, even each other, so I don't really mind.

Anyway, last Sunday Kylie's mum drove them all to the designer outlets in Kildare Village to go shopping. When I asked why they didn't invite me, Kylie said there wasn't room in the car, but I know she was lying 'cause her mum has one of those SUVs with three rows of seats. I said I felt really left out, but she told me to get a grip and stop being a baby.

It's not the first time they've done things without me. And sometimes they ignore me in school and walk straight past me in the corridor. Sometimes I wonder if they're real friends at all.

What do you think, Clover and Amy? Am I being paranoid, or are they way out of line?

Trusting you to tell me the truth,

Frizzy, 13

XXX

"Poor Frizzy," I say, putting the letter down.

Clover looks up from her nails. "What advice would you give her, Beanie?"

"Easy peasy, lemon squeezy," I say. "First of all

those girls — Kylie, Danni, and Cheryl, or whatever their real names are — sound more like frenemies than real friends."

"Excellent, Beanie. Anything else?"

"Yes. I'd tell her to forget the backstabbing three-some and hang out with Susie more, who sounds kind of sweet. Loyal too. I'd tell her a true friend is worth hanging on to, no matter what."

"Good thinking, Beanie." Clover sounds impressed. "Couldn't do better myself. You've rightly nailed that one. Now try the next letter. It's a bit more complicated." Her eyes dart away. Is it my imagination or does she seem nervous?

Dear Clover and Amy,

I could really do with your advice. I'm supposed to be starting college any day now, but I'm petrified. The problem is that on the outside I appear ultra-confident and together, but inside I'm Silly Putty. I find it hard to trust people and to make new friends. I had a best friend in school, but eventually she showed her true colors and I got my fingers not just burned but completely bushfire torched—which leads me to the second problem. This girl is at the same college, taking similar classes, and I'm dreading bumping into her. Seeing her will remind me of the whole sorry affair, time after time.

I'm tempted not to bother with college at all and to stick with writing for the *Goss*.

What do you think, Beanie?

Seriously down,

Clover X

♥ Chapter 6

"Clover! I had no idea you were so worried. You should have said something. It's your old friend Cliona, right? The girl who betrayed you?"

Clover stops painting her nails, twists the tiny brush back into the bottle, and looks at me, her eyes twinkling with tears. "What if I bump into her in college?" Her eyes widen. "Or *him*? I'd die."

"Him? Who are you talking about, Clover?"

She gives a deep, raggedy sigh. "Kendall." Tears start spilling down her cheeks. "Seeing them together will kill me."

"Together?"

She nods, wiping the tears away with her fingers. "Cliona and Kendall were seeing each other, behind my back. That's why Cliona and I aren't friends anymore. I lost my boyfriend *and* my best friend in one fell swoop. I thought I was over it, but it still hurts so much."

I'm genuinely shocked. Clover and Cliona were like me and Mills — inseparable. And Kendall was Clover's first proper boyfriend; they were together for over three years. I can't believe he'd do such a thing, especially after everything Clover went through. Clover's mum (my gran) died nearly five years ago, and Kendall came to the funeral. He sat beside Clover and held her hand during the service — stayed with her the whole day, in fact. I remember thinking, *When I'm older, I want a boyfriend just like Lucas Kendall.*

"I can't believe you didn't tell me he cheated on you!" I say. "You said it was a mutual decision, that your lives were going in different directions."

"I lied," she says simply. "I couldn't face telling you the truth. The fact is he betrayed me — they both did — the night of his seventeenth birthday. Kendall was having this huge party in a tent in his garden. A DJ and everything. It wasn't supposed to start till eight, but I decided I'd get there early to surprise him. I wanted to give him his present before everyone started arriving. I knew he was getting a car for his birthday, so I'd bought him a GPS. Cost me a fortune. Anyway, I went straight round the back and walked into the tent, and there they were: Kendall and Cliona, their arms wrapped around each other, kissing."

I gasp. "No! That's horrible."

"Tell me about it. I felt like I'd been stabbed. I got such a fright, I dropped the GPS. They must have heard it smash on the floor, because they both spun around. And do you know what Cliona did when she saw me, Beanie? She smiled. Just for a split second — but it was still a smile. I think she *wanted* me to catch them. Wanted for it all to be out in the open."

"And then?" I ask, transfixed.

"Kendall started apologizing: saying how sorry he was, how he'd never meant for it to happen. I asked him how long it had been going on, and Cliona answered for him. A month, she said. And then I really lost it. I told him he was a useless good-for-nothing, and I threw the shattered GPS at him and stormed out."

"Yikes. Did you hit him?"

"No, but I wish I had. Stupid pig."

I whistle and shake my head. "That's quite a story, Clover. I guessed you must have had some sort of falling-out with Cliona — one minute you guys were best buddies, and then you suddenly stopped talking completely — but you never wanted to discuss it, so I figured the subject was off-limits. But this . . ." I trail off. "It's horrible. She's some piece of work. And as for Kendall, I don't know what to say. I know how much you liked him." I put my arm around her shoulders.

"I loved him, Beanie. Really, really *loved* him." She leans against me and starts sobbing; her eyes are waterfalls of tears, and snot is coming from her nose. I've never seen her in such a state — it's very unnerving.

"It'll be OK, Clover." I hand her a tissue from my bedside table.

"How?" she wails. "How will it be OK? Knowing every time I turn a corner they might be there, holding hands, just waiting to laugh at me, is driving me crazy."

"Maybe they're not together anymore."

She sniffs and blows her nose. "They are."

"How do you know?"

"Headcount. I've been checking their profiles." (Headcount is the new Facebook. You can find out all kinds of things about people, and, unlike Facebook, you don't have to be a "friend" to search the info.)

"I'm so sorry, Clover." I give her a squeeze, not knowing what else to do.

"Me too." Her eyes well up again, and she dabs

at them. Then she takes a deep breath. "Funny — it's the first time I've actually cried about the whole Kendall drama-rama. What a mess. It's too late to change colleges, and besides Trinity has one of the best English courses in the country. But seeing the two of them holding hands in the corridor might just tip me over the edge. I really don't want to go. Any advice for me?"

"But you have Brains now," I point out gently.

"I know. It still hurts, though."

"You can't shipwreck your whole college career because of two nasty, deceitful eejits, Clover. You just can't. If you drop out, they've won. Maybe it will always hurt a bit, but you have to move on."

"Move on? How exactly, Beanie? The mere thought of bumping into them makes my stomach churn."

She looks so sad and anxious — I know I have to do something. The question is what? This one has me stumped — maybe some problems really are too big to be fixed. But this is Clover's life we're talking about. I have to help her!

"I'll think of something," I tell her. "And that's a promise. But in the meantime, you're going to college, and that's that. I'll drag you in myself, if I have to."

"At least my toes look bootiful," she says with a glum smile.

Her mobile bleeps then, and she reads the message. *"Siúcra ducra"*— she slaps her head with her palm—"the teen surf gods photo shoot! I was supposed to be on Killiney Beach ten minutes ago. Would you be a doll and write up Frizzy's answer and file it straight to Saffy when you're finished? I'm so over deadline, it's scary biscuits. You have Saffy's e-mail address, right?" She slides her feet carefully into her flip-flops. "I'll be forever yours, Beanie. I'm so behind with everything. Saffy wanted this surfing piece like yesterday, and I haven't even done the research yet."

I roll my eyes and smile. "OK, just this once."

I'm actually quite excited. It's the first time Clover's let me file a piece without checking it over first.

"Coola boola. Sorry for burdening you with all my woes. You feeling a bit brighter yourself now, babes?"

I nod—compared to Clover's problems, mine are gnat-size. "Thanks for coming over."

"You're more than welcome. And I'm sure Mills will snap out of it soon—try not to fret." She kisses her fingers and waves them at me. "Toodle-oo, babes." She runs out of the door, then stops and dashes back in again.

"I told you about Friday night, right?" she asks.

47 ♥

"No."

She gives a laugh. "I'm such a scatterbrain at the moment. I'll pick you up at seven. Tell Sylvie I'm taking you out for pizza. But wear something hot! And there's a slot for Mills, if you can tempt her away from lover-boy." She lowers her voice. "And put on your dancing shoes. The girls are going capital O-U-T!"

♥ Chapter 7

By Friday morning I know I have to tackle Mills over Bailey, and the sooner the better — we're on the way to school, and she's in the middle of yet another monologue, and unless I stop her, I'm going to jump in front of a bus.

"Do you think Bailey would look better in black or blue?" she's saying in the usual daydreamy voice she uses when she's talking about him. "I spotted a really nice shirt in the *Goss*. They did this 'Dress Your Boyfriend' fashion spread and—"

"Mills! All this Bailey stuff is doing my head in. Please, you have to cease and desist."

"What Bailey stuff?"

I put my hands over my face and groan. Clover's right. Mills *is* delusional.

"Mills, Mr. Otis is your sole topic of conversation 24/7. You talk about nothing else."

"That's rubbish," she says, but from the blush creeping across her cheeks, I can tell she knows it's true.

"And I wish you'd stop with the kissing in front of me. It's embarrassing."

"We never kiss in front of you, Amy . . . Well, hardly ever."

"Mills! Come on. The D4s are calling you Leech Lips."

"Leech Lips? That's disgusting. And most unfair."

I sigh. "Mills, I know you're crazy about Bailey, but you're going to have to cool it in school. And it might be worth playing just a little bit hard to get, don't you think?"

She gasps. "Do you think he's going off me? Did Seth say something?"

"No, of course not. But you guys spend so much time together, it's not healthy."

Her back stiffens. "That's just your opinion, Amy."

Now she's really starting to annoy me. "For the record," I say, "Clover thinks you're behaving like a sap."

"What do you mean?"

"Dumping your mates once you have a boyfriend

is classic D4 behavior, she said, and utterly beneath you."

Mills swallows and looks away. I can tell she doesn't like what she's hearing, but it might just be sinking in. Mills thinks Clover is *the* expert when it comes to love.

"Do you agree with Clover, Amy?" she asks finally.

"Yes," I say firmly.

"Have I really been that obsessed?"

"And then some."

She plays with her ponytail, flicking it around a finger. "I guess I have some making up to do." One of the nice things about Mills is that she admits her mistakes. "How about shopping tomorrow?" she suggests. "Just the two of us."

"I'm at Dad's this weekend. And I'm going out with Clover tonight. But she said you're welcome to tag along. We're meeting at my place at seven. She won't tell me where we're going—but knowing Clover, it's bound to be fun. Will you come? Please?"

"I said I'd go to a movie with Bailey tonight. There's this horror thing he wants to see."

I stare at her. Hasn't she been listening to a word I've said? "Mills, you hate scary movies more than I do."

"Don't say a word to Bailey—I told him I was a

big fan. And besides, I can't cancel now. Bailey goes mad if I try to rearrange things at the last minute."

"Fine," I say in a clipped voice, and then start marching toward the train station.

Mills runs after me and grabs my arm. "Slow down, Amy. What's wrong?"

"If you don't know, then I'm not telling you."

"Don't be like that. I'm sorry, but I promised Bailey . . ." She trails off.

"As I said, it's fine. Look, I just realized I forgot my classics homework, and Miss Sketchberry will have a fit. You go on — no point in both of us being late."

"Are you sure? I don't want to leave you, but —" Mills hates being late for school; she has her heart set on being Head Girl.

"See you later." I walk back toward my house, blinking back angry tears. I don't go all the way home but wait at the corner of my street to put enough distance between us to ensure we're on different trains. Bailey normally catches that train too, and right now I don't think I could bear to watch another episode of *The Mills and Bailey Show.*

That evening I'm surprised to find Mills on my door-step just before seven.

"What are you doing here?" I ask her, a little

crossly. "Thought you were going to the movies with love's young dream."

"I thought I'd go out with my best bud instead. I rang Clover this afternoon, and she said it was 'Coolio, babes.'"

"Then she'll also have told you that I intend to park my bum on the sofa all night." I'd had a lousy day at school since Seth wasn't in — sometimes he stays off to go to the hospital with Polly — and I'd spent most of the time trying to avoid Mills and Bailey. I rang Clover earlier and told her I wasn't in the mood for going out.

But Mills is having none of it. "I told her we were both definitely on for it. Said I'd talk you round. So you'd better get changed. Our Clover taxi will be here any second."

"Weren't you listening?" I cross my arms grumpily. "I'm not going, and there's nothing you can do to change my mind."

"Actually there is" — she smiles smugly — "you've left me with no alternative: I'm calling Mouse. All for one and one for all — remember?"

I squeal despite my bad mood. "No! That's so unfair. I haven't called Mouse on you in years."

"Ha! I'm calling Mouse and that's that. Throw on your new skinny jeans — they look fab."

I glare at her, but she's won and she knows it.

"Go on, Ames," she cajoles. "You know you secretly want to. You're just being stubborn."

"You're unbelievable, Mills, you know that?"

She just smiles and mouths "Mouse" at me.

Calling Mouse is so underhanded, I think as I stomp up the stairs. When we were little, Mills had this videotape called *The Three Mouseketeers,* and we both adored it. One day we were snuggled up on the sofa in Mills's house eating bowls of ice cream, with Mills's duvet pulled over our legs. *The Three Mouseketeers* had just finished. "All for one and one for all," Mills said, swinging her empty spoon in the air like a sword the way the little mice did.

"Friends forever," I said, waving my own spoon and quoting the mice: "'Whatever is asked in the name of Mouse must be obeyed. 'Cause we are the Mouseketeers.'"

And then we swore an oath of friendship — just like the mice. And for years we used to call "Mouse" on each other. I can't believe she used it on me today — although she is right: I am dying to find out what Clover has in store for us. I can feel my bad mood lifting already.

* * *

"We're running a bit late, so hold on to your hats," Clover says as she speeds away from my house at twenty past seven. She's a pretty nifty driver, fast but safe. She'd rock that celebrity lap competition on *Top Gear* — whup Simon Cowell, for instance, into the tarmac. Last year Gramps gave her a track session for her birthday, and she loved it — she roared around Mondello Park like a pro.

Mills chatters away in the car, telling Clover about Bailey. She really is oblivious sometimes; she's clearly forgotten all about our earlier conversation. At least she's here, I guess. Now and then, Clover catches my eye in the rearview mirror and gives me a gentle smile.

"Clover, does Brains ever go quiet?" Mills asks. "Like he's thinking about something?" (Brains is Clover's boyfriend. He's in a band called the Golden Lions and is super cool.)

"All the time," Clover says. "Especially when he's in the middle of writing a new song. I have to wave my hand in front of his eyes to snap him out of it."

"Bailey writes songs," Mills says. "He's amazing. Wait till I tell you about—"

"Let's throw on some tunes," Clover says quickly. She puts on the Golden Lions CD that Brains had cut especially for her, cranks it up loud, and starts seat dancing. That shuts Mills up.

Clover tucks her Mini into a parking lot in Temple Bar, and we walk through the cobbled back streets, up Crane Lane, and take a right, onto Dame Street. The evening traffic is heavy, buses and cars trundle by, and the metallic exhaust fumes catch at the back of my throat, making me cough. The street is jammed with people, and we have to step around a clump of American tourists staring at a map in the middle of the pavement. Mills insists on helping them locate "Kelly's Book" aka the Book of Kells, while Clover and I jiggle around impatiently.

Once outside the Olympia Theatre, Clover spreads her arms out and says, "Ta-da!"

I stare at her. "The theater? Tell me it's not Shakespeare, Clover. Miss Bingley took us to *Hamlet* last year, and it was a snoozefest."

"No kidding," Mills adds. "I mean, 'To be or not to be'? Seriously, who cares? I wouldn't mind seeing *Romeo and Juliet*, though. So romantic."

Clover laughs. "It's not Shakespeare, I promise. Look!" She points at the poster to the right of the door. The image of a big yellow sun looks familiar. Hang on — it's a lion's head, not a sun.

"The Golden Lions!" I squeal. "Brains is playing here? It's a huge venue."

"I know," she says proudly. "Biggest capacity yet. Brains thinks they've reached a tipping point, whatever that means. They're getting loads of radio play. And we have super-cool seats, courtesy of the man himself. But for goodness' sake, don't tell your mothers. That especially goes for you, Bean Machine. Sylvie would kill for your ticket. I know it's cruel, but I just couldn't face her embarrassing mummy dancing. And the screaming — my ears rang for days after the last Take That gig. She was worse than the teenyboppers. Ready, girls?"

Mills is so excited, she's squirming like there's ice down her back. "Yes!" she shrieks.

"Abso-doodle-lutely," I say, giving Clover a huge hug. "As always, Clover Wildgust, you diamond rock!"

♥ Chapter 8

Everywhere I look, there are excited fans in yellow T-shirts singing snatches of Golden Lions songs. I can't believe Brains and his bandmates are becoming real rock stars. Mills and I weave our way through the crowd and follow Clover into the lobby of the theater, past the ticket collector, down a busy corridor, and through a doorway to the left, and then up lots and lots of red-carpeted stairs. Finally we head down another narrower corridor with old-fashioned red-and-black flocked wallpaper. A bank of doors stretches out in front of us. Clover pulls one open. Inside is our very own box overlooking the packed auditorium and just a few feet away from the stage. The music hits us, and Mills goes into shock. "Holy moly" is all she can say, over and over again, as she runs her hand over the red-velvet drapes and then stares down at the crowd and dark stage below us. The stage curtains are open, but there's no sign of the band yet.

As we take our seats, the background music starts to fade out. The stage lights power up, illuminating the drum kit and the guitars sitting stiff and upright in their stands like toy soldiers, and the crowd cheers. Suddenly the Golden Lions, minus Brains, run onto the stage, waving at the audience. The whole Olympia Theatre explodes with excitement.

Barra sits down behind his kit and spins his drumsticks in the air. "Yeah!" he hollers, and starts beating out a crazily fast drum loop with his muscular arms.

Diablo, a black fedora pulled over his strawberry-blond hair, joins in on keyboards, and finally Felix comes in on lead guitar. Felix starts lunging forward and backward, lost in the music — and the crowd goes even wilder. Felix has true rock-god looks — piercing green eyes, sweeping eyelashes that could bat for Ireland, full lips (complete with tiny white scar near the cupid's bow), and night-black hair that flops over his face. He's wearing a black skull T-shirt, skinny jeans, and biker boots — and I can't take my eyes off him.

"Where's Brains?" I ask Clover loudly over the music.

She cups her hand around her mouth and whispers, "Patience, Grasshopper," in my ear.

And then there's an earth-shattering roar from the back of the theater. Brains is standing on the edge of the upper-circle balcony in gold lamé trousers and a white shirt unbuttoned to his waist. "We are the Golden Lions!" he yells into his headset microphone. "Hear us roar!" Then he jumps off the edge of the balcony.

I scream, and Clover grips my hand, hard. "Brains!" she shrieks.

But he doesn't fall. Instead he flies through the air, on what must be an invisible wire, toward the stage. He almost collides with Felix, who has to jump out of the way.

"Lions! Lions! Lions!" the crowd thunders.

Me and Mills and Clover join in: clapping our hands, stomping our feet, and chanting, "Brains! Brains! Brains!"

Then Diablo plays the opening bars to "Caroline"—my favorite Golden Lions song. Even though they haven't gotten a record deal yet, the song's been all over the radio and everyone here seems to know it.

Brains belts out the first line over the cheers and applause. "Where have you been all my life, baby? I've been searching for a girl like you. A girl I can hold, touch, love."

His eyes scan the boxes looking for Clover as he sings the next line. "A girl I can trust with my heart." He thumps his chest with his fist. "My torn, abused heart. Are you that girl? Everyone . . ." He punches the air, and the whole theater joins in as one. "Car-o-line. Are you that girl? Car-o-line."

I smile. The song's about Clover, but Brains couldn't get her name to fit the music. He tried Clover-belle but said it made her sound like a pet donkey.

Clover is beaming, her eyes locked on Brains's face, tears rolling down her cheeks. Happy tears this time. I can't imagine how it must feel to have a song written just for you — but it must feel pretty amazing. I squeeze her hand, and she squeezes back.

"They're going to be huge, Clover," I yell. "Everyone loves them! This is just the start."

"I know." She beams at me, her eyes watery with emotion. "Isn't it exciting?"

When the song ends, the roof nearly lifts with the applause.

"What an atmosphere," Mills says as the intro

to the next song plays and the clapping dies down a little. "I love this place. And these boxes are super cool. I feel like a princess up here." She looks across at one of the other boxes, and her face freezes.

Staring back at us, his arm thrown around Annabelle Hamilton's shoulders, is Bailey Otis. And from his startled expression and the way he quickly pulls his arm away from her, it's clear he's spotted us too.

It's car-crash viewing. Mills looks as if her world's just stopped spinning. She crumples against me.

"This one is for anyone who's ever had their heart stomped on," Brains says from the stage as I hold Mills up. "It's called 'Burning Love.'"

"I have to . . . Out." Mills staggers toward the door.

"Is she OK?" Clover shouts over the music.

"She's too hot. She needs air. Back in a sec."

I follow Mills outside. She has slid down the wall, her arms hugging her legs and her head pressed against her kneecaps. She's crying so hard, her back is heaving up and down. I crouch down beside her.

"He did go a bit funny when I said I was spending the evening with you instead, but I didn't expect . . ." she says through her tears. "What's wrong with me? Am I not good enough? I shouldn't have canceled on him. He hates it when I do that . . . But did it have to be Annabelle Hamilton?"

"I'm so sorry, Mills. I don't know what to say. It doesn't make any sense. Bailey's obviously not who we thought he was. Don't let him spoil our night, though. Come back inside."

She shakes her head. "I can't. It's too humiliating."

I stay with her, stroking her head and listening to the muffled sound of "Burning Love" coming through the closed door. After a few minutes, the song ends and there's more ecstatic applause.

Mills sighs. "You go inside, Ames. You shouldn't miss the whole gig because of me."

"There'll be other gigs. I'm not going to leave you out here on your own."

"Thanks, Ames. I don't deserve you."

I nudge her with my shoulder. "Yes, you do. You're my best friend, Mills, and besties stick together, no matter what. All for one and one for all, remember?"

She smiles and nods, but the smile doesn't reach her heartbroken eyes.

"We can still listen to the music," I say. "And Clover said there's an intermission. Maybe you'll feel strong enough to watch the second half."

"Maybe." She doesn't sound convinced.

* * *

"You OK, Mills?" Clover asks, walking out of the box at intermission. "Should I ring your mum?"

"No, I'm feeling a bit better now."

"Are you sure? You look terrible. Your eyes are all red and blotchy."

I figure I should just tell Clover the truth — but Mills gets in there first. "Bailey," she says, "was in one of the other boxes with a girl from school. He's cheating on me with one of the D4s."

Clover says something very rude under her breath and then sighs. "Poor you. Sometimes boys can be evil. Would meeting the band help cheer you up? I have a special invitation from Mr. Showbiz himself to rendezvous backstage. What do you think?"

Mills manages a smile. "Yes, please."

Clover grins. "Good. And we'll do a quick pit stop in the ladies' to cover up those old blotches. I never travel without my trusty makeup kit — just in case. This way, troops."

After visiting the loos, we walk down the corridor to the left of the stage. Clover has a word with the Billy Goats Gruff security man, who nods, stands aside, and opens the door for her.

"Follow me, *chiquitas*," Clover says.

I'm not sure what I was expecting — trays of posh

sandwiches, pink cupcakes, champagne in silver buckets — but I think I've been watching too many Hollywood movies. The backstage room is pretty plain — two sofas, some plastic chairs, and a table with some bottles of water, paper napkins, Pringles, and ham-and-cheese sandwiches. The room smells of stale cigarette smoke and sweat.

Brains bounces over, throws his arms around Clover's waist, and lifts her off the floor. "What did you think, babes?"

Clover laughs. "Unhand me, beast, you're all sticky."

He plonks her back down.

"You were fan-dabby-dozy," she goes on enthusiastically. "Best set ever. 'Caroline' was amazing. And 'Burning Love,' genius." They start discussing the crowd's reaction to the playlist, song by song.

Mills is standing against the wall, looking glum. *Siúcra*. I want to do something to help her, but what? I'm so angry with Bailey for spoiling all this for her. What is he playing at?

I touch Clover's arm. "Can I talk to you for a second? Sorry to interrupt, Brains. And loving it so far."

He smiles and tips his fingers to his head in a salute. "No worries, little lady. She's all yours. And the second half will be even better. Sure as dogs have

65 ♥

fleas." He breaks into a deep, growly Johnny Cash accent. "We'll be rockin' this joint like it's Folsom Prison." If being good at accents is a basis for a relationship, then he and Clover are truly made for each other.

"What's up, jelly tot?" Clover asks as soon as Brains has wandered off toward the food.

"I don't want Mills to miss the second half, so I'm going to confront Bailey. See what I can do. At the very least it might stop him from kissing Annabelle in front of Mills. Wish me luck, and keep an eye on her for me."

She smiles. "You're a good *amigo*, Bean Machine. I'll be rooting for you."

I walk back to the main hallway and up the stairs to the boxes opposite ours. I find what I hope is the right door and stop outside it to take a deep breath, and then I pull it open before I chicken out. I peer in, expecting to see Bailey and Annabelle sucking face — but Bailey's alone, playing with his mobile.

He looks up as I walk in. "Amy."

"Bailey."

We stare at each other. He looks awkward and embarrassed. He keeps running his hands through his dark hair and moving his fringe across his face, as if protecting himself from my scowl.

"I wasn't expecting to see you here," he says eventually. "Or Mills. Is she OK?"

"How can you be such a lying, cheating pig?" I say, anger rippling up and down my spine. "No, she's not OK. She's heartbroken! I can't believe you're flaunting Annabelle in her face like that. What are you doing with her, anyway? What's going on?"

He shrugs. "Annabelle's dad got free tickets. She asked me this afternoon after Mills blew me off, and I said yes. I was pleased Mills didn't want to see me tonight actually. It gave me space. Made me realize it was all getting a bit serious. A bit too intense. I really like Mills — she's amazing — but she's too . . . Oh, I don't know . . . It's hard to explain . . . Anyway, it wouldn't work, not long term."

I stare at him, flabbergasted. "What are you talking about? You two were all over each other on Wednesday. You should have talked to her, not . . ." — I grasp for the words — "not . . . this. And not with Annabelle Hamilton! I think you're a coward, Bailey Otis. You're lucky to have a girlfriend like Mills. She's the most loyal person I know. She'd never treat you like dirt or abandon you. You should be ashamed of yourself."

He winces as if he's been hit, but he doesn't say anything and something flickers across his face—

anguish, fear, pain? Our eyes connect, and in them I see Mum at her lowest: after Dad had moved out and demanded a legal separation. I see someone who is crushed and alone, and it frightens me. He dips his head, his hair closing over his face like a dark curtain.

I put my hand on his and try one final time. "Bailey, talk to me. Is there something—"

"Would you look what the cat dragged in . . ." Annabelle says, appearing behind me. I turn around to see a nasty sneer on her face.

Bailey pulls his hand away from under my palm as if scalded.

"Admiring our box, Amy?" Annabelle goes on. "It's far bigger than yours. My dad has, like, amazing connections." (It's exactly the same size as our box, but I can't be bothered arguing with her.) She picks an imaginary piece of fluff off Bailey's black T-shirt and then leaves her hand resting on his arm, like a territorial guard dog.

I look at Bailey, and he holds my gaze for a moment, then slides his eyes toward the stage, where a man is changing one of the guitars.

"Five minutes, ladies and gentlemen," a voice rings out loudly over the sound system. "Please take your seats."

"You heard the man, Amy," Annabelle says, pointing at the door. "Back to your pigpen. Don't stay where you're not wanted."

I try to get Bailey to look at me again, but he won't meet my eyes. I leave to the sound of Annabelle's tittering, feeling hurt, confused, and disappointed. What on earth has happened to Bailey? It's baffling.

When I get back to our own box, Clover's sitting there alone. "You all right?" she asks.

I nod. "But Bailey's not. It's all off with Mills, according to him, and it looks like he doesn't even have the guts to tell her himself. Where is she, anyway — in the loo?"

"No, she's about to show that Bailey creature what he's missing. Remember Frizzy and Susie?"

"The girls from the *Goss* letter?"

"Yup. Frizzy e-mailed me to say thanks for the advice. We got chatting, and she mentioned that her so-called friends were going to a gig and hadn't invited her. She said that was it as far as she was concerned: she wasn't hanging out with them ever again. Guess what gig."

I smile. I can see where this is going. "It wouldn't happen to be the Golden Lions at the Olympia Theatre, would it?"

"Got it in one, Beanie. So I arranged something

special for Frizzy and Susie with Brains — something to give those frenemies a taste of their own medicine. And Mills is going to join them!"

Suddenly the lights in the auditorium dim, the stage lights come up, and the Golden Lions run on, followed by two girls in matching *Twilight* T-shirts; one is small and blond, and the other is taller with a head of amazing red curly hair. It must be Frizzy! And right behind them is Mills. She looks a mixture of mortified and over the moon: her cheeks are pink, her eyes glistening.

"Mills!" I shriek down at her.

She waves up at us, and I blow her a kiss.

"What are they doing on the stage?" I ask Clover, bewildered.

She shakes her head. "So impatient, Grasshopper. All will be revealed."

"On the tambourine for one song only," Brains hollers. "We have our Lionettes, the coolest rock chicks ever — Mills, Susie, and Frizzy."

The opening bars of "Forest Fire" ring out, and the three girls tap tambourines on their hips. The crowd cheers wildly.

I shriek again. "No way!"

Clover hoots with laughter. "I thought Mills might as well join in the fun."

I peer across the auditorium at Bailey and Annabelle. Annabelle is frozen statue-still, her mouth a huge O while Bailey's eyes are glued to Mills. That'll show him — Mills is worth millions of any D4.

I clutch Clover's arm in excitement. "I heart you so much for arranging this, Clover."

"You're so welcome, Beanie." She grins. "No one messes with my girls, ever. Now, let's cheer them all on."

We punch our fists in the air and chant, "Lionettes! Lionettes! Lionettes!"

♥ Chapter 9

"Do you notice anything different about me?" I ask Dad, flicking the front of my hair a little to give him a clue. It's Saturday afternoon, and we've brought my baby sister Gracie to the Dublin Zoo. A father-daughter trip, Dad called it, but I think it was just a ruse to get away from Pauline, Shelly's ultra-painful mum. If I had to pick the one person I'd least like to be stuck on a desert island with, Pauline would be right up there, along with Annabelle Hamilton and Dad's annoying new wife, Shelly.

Pauline and Shelly are very similar: they are both whippet thin, with huge white teeth, china-blue baby-doll eyes, and an entire wardrobe of tacky white and gold clothes.

Dad tears his eyes away from the tigers to look me up and down. "New jeans?" he tries with a shrug.

"Dad! I got my hair cut this morning. I've got a fringe." I do jazz hands on either side of my forehead. "Ta-da!"

He smiles. "So you do. Makes you look older."

I grin back. "Correct answer, Pops. Mum thinks so too." I'm still a bit unsure whether I'll keep it, though—unless I straighten the fringe every morning, I suspect it'll look a mess. And unlike the D4s, I'm not interested in daily primping just for school.

We leave the tiger enclosure, and Dad pushes Gracie's top-of-the-range Bugaboo toward the monkey island. I walk along beside him.

"Want to push your little sis?" he asks.

"Later maybe." I'm getting a kick out of watching Dad try to negotiate the crowds. In his camel-colored cashmere coat and pointy-toe Prada boots, he looks a little out of place, like a male model playing "dad" in a Ralph Lauren photo shoot. Most of the other dads are wearing practical rain jackets, zipped over their potbellies.

We watch the monkeys gibbering and swinging from the ropes for a few minutes, and then I notice that two spider monkeys are holding hands and spinning around. "They look like they're dancing," I say, pointing at them.

Dad smiles. "So they do. That reminds me, my bank's sponsoring a ballet this Christmas featuring Mills's sister. Cool, huh?"

I look at him in surprise. "In Budapest?"

Claire Starr moved to Budapest when she was fifteen to train in their state ballet school, and now she's a full-blown ballerina. Mills doesn't talk about her very often — Claire isn't very good at keeping in touch with her family, and I think it's a bit of a sore point. She hasn't been home for two years.

"No, Dublin. They're doing *Romeo and Juliet* in the Grand Canal Theatre, and Claire's headlining. They're calling her the Irish Ballerina. Great marketing ploy, eh? It was all a bit hush-hush until the sponsorship deal was finalized last week."

It's strange Mills hasn't mentioned it yet, but maybe Claire wasn't allowed to tell anyone until the funding was sorted. Ballets cost an absolute fortune to stage apparently, and without a big sponsor they just don't happen.

"As part of the deal, all the traders are getting a bunch of free tickets for the opening night," Dad goes on. "Ballet puts me to sleep, though. Want my seats?"

"Abso-doodle-lutely! Can I bring Mills and Clover?" Mills will probably go with her mum and dad, anyway, but I'm sure she'd be happy to watch it twice, and maybe she could get us backstage to see all the dancers. Clover says male ballet dancers are hot up close and personal (she had a brief dalliance with one before she met Brains), and I want to see if she's right.

"Sure. You can bring Sylvie along too."

"Thanks, Dad."

Gracie wakes then and starts to make little mewing noises.

"Better get this little lady home," Dad says. He checks his watch. "Hopefully Pauline will be at the gym by now. The sooner that woman flies back to Portugal on her broomstick the better. She's doing my head in. She really stirred things up this morning over breakfast. Asked me why Shelly wasn't invited to your mum's bachelorette party! I don't think it had even occurred to Shelly to be miffed — but she is now."

"Is Pauline deranged? Shelly's the last person Mum would want within a million miles of her party."

"I know that and you know that. Anyway, don't worry; I set Pauline straight. Told her it was just close friends and family. Shelly still had a puss on her, though, so I had to promise to take her shopping to make up for it."

Phew! Mum's bachelorette party is already getting far too complicated for my liking. Dave has invited his prissy sister, Prue, along, and her idea of outlandish is wearing a red velvet hairband instead of her usual navy blue one.

Gracie cries all the way to the exit, where Dad makes a big deal out of maneuvering her buggy out the gate. Honestly, you'd swear he was driving a bus. As we walk toward the car, Gracie finally goes quiet again, and I peer in at her. She's snoozing peacefully, her nose wriggling like a rabbit's, her mouth making little sucking motions, like she's pulling on an imaginary bottle.

"How are the party plans coming along, anyway?" Dad asks. "Is there a theme?"

I worry my lip. I'm a little concerned about Clover's ideas, to be honest. Mum said simple — but some of it is looking Brains-worthy eccentric.

"The theme is *Sex and the City*, Irish style," I tell him. "Manhattan meets Dublin."

Dad laughs. "Sounds brilliant. I'm sure Sylvie will love it."

I hope he's right.

♥ Chapter 10

"I do love teacher-training days," I say to Clover on Monday morning. We're marching across the rugby field at Trinity College, and I'm swinging my arms like a soldier on parade.

"I feel bad about dragging you out of bed so early on a day off, Beanie," Clover says. She then gives a jaw-cracking yawn. Clover isn't a morning person. "Are you sure you want to do this?"

"Yes!" I say, stepping over a divot. "But everyone else is walking on the path. Are we allowed to walk on the grass?"

And as though in answer to my question, a short man in dark blue overalls waves a rake at us and shouts, "Oy, off the grass!"

"Apparently not." Clover grabs my arm, and we run toward the path, laughing.

We join the stream of students flowing toward Front Square. It's day one of Freshers' Week, and from the excited chatter of a bunch of D4s in flicky mini-kilts and brand-spanking new Uggs in front of us, I'd say it's a REALLY BIG DEAL!

"What societies are you joining, Amber?" one of them asks a tall girl with long, perfectly straightened mink-colored hair. (The D4s have all gone mink this season—it's the latest thing, apparently. Smacks of beige to me.)

"Field Hockey Club, obviously—they, like, so need me," Amber answers, her haughty voice dripping with confidence. "I have been capped for Ireland after all." It's clear from the way the others have stopped chattering and are listening to her intently that she's Queen Bee. "Also Drama Society. And the college magazine. My second cousin's the editor. We're, like, Siamese-twins close. Practically best friends."

"Which cousin's that?" a dark-haired girl asks. "Tiffany?"

"No, Tiffany's taking a cooking course in Ballymaloe, remember? Where they send all the Leaving Cert rejects. It's costing Uncle Seb a fortune. He says if she can whack out a decent steak, she might just bag herself a rich husband. It's the only hope for her. No, I'm talking about Cliona. She's the editor, you dim sim."

I give a tiny gasp. "She's not talking about *your* Cliona, is she?" I whisper to Clover.

"You eavesdropping too, Beanie?" Clover nudges me before shaking her head. "It can't be, though. Cliona might be a wagon of the highest order, but she's a goth, and a goth being besties with a D4 is a step too far."

"Cliona's an inspiration," Amber is saying. "It's the first time a second year's been made editor." She lifts her hair off her neck, letting it fall back across her shoulders in a wave, and even several feet away, I get a whiff of expensive shampoo.

The D4 pack has reached some concrete steps to the right of a large modern building, and Amber suddenly stops dead. She lifts her hand like a traffic warden and swings round to face her tribe. (She's much prettier than I'd imagined, with a heart-shaped face and wide-set hazel eyes, like a cat's.) "Halt!" she says. "Makeup check."

At her command, all the girls whip out cosmetic bags and hand mirrors and begin topping up their gloop.

Clover stops too and pretends to study her

mobile phone. I linger beside her, watching the D4s from the corner of my eye.

"Remember, first impressions are, like, crucial," Amber says, snapping her compact closed and slipping it back into her leather satchel. "Today is the most important day in your college career. Hit the stands with pride. We are Mounties, girls. We belong here. Heads up, shoulders back, boobs out. Let's show them what we're made of."

And like a plague of rich, privileged locusts, they swarm up the steps, past a bronze globe sculpture, and into the college building.

Clover stares after them. "I can't spend four years surrounded by Mount Rackville monsters, Beanie. Girls from that school think they're so superior, and I hate the way they call themselves Mounties. I think I'll just register, grab my student ID card, and then head in to the *Goss* office and get some work done."

I look at Clover, but her eyes quickly dart away from mine. She seems nervous, agitated.

"Can we just have a quick look at some of the society stands?" I say. "There's free pizza at the Students' Union, and the engineers have a bungee run. Pretty please?"

We flicked through the Freshers' Week program on the DART on the way in, and some of the societies sound fantastic. I know if I can just get her to look around, she'll be excited again. I won't let her be put off by a bunch of D4s!

She sighs and rolls her eyes at me. "OK, fine. But first I have to register in the exam hall and pick up my student card. You need an ID card before you can join any of the societies, anyway. Which way, bloodhound?"

"Follow the crowd, I guess." I point at a group of Crombies (the male equivalents of D4s). They are all in matching jeans and Abercrombie & Fitch Ts and are jostling one another with their broad rugby player shoulders.

"It's a sad day when I have to trail Crombies — but I guess you're right, Beanie."

We tail them but keep our distance. After walking through a narrow opening, we find ourselves in a huge cobbled square that is thronging with noisy students. It's also heaving with stands — some are tented, some are decorated with colored banners, and all are manned by students in hoodies or tops printed with their society's name.

We sniggle our way through the bodies. The air is thick with sweat, beer fumes, and aftershave so strong you can taste it. (The Crombies have obviously been dousing themselves as usual.) There's a queue snaking outside one of the Georgian buildings to the left, so we weave our way in and out of the crush toward it. The sign on the wall says "NEW STUDENT REGISTRATION." Bingo!

Luckily the queue is moving quickly, and within minutes we find ourselves inside, where we join another busy queue to the right, marked "ARTS." The building is ancient, with huge wooden doors like a church and a soaring ceiling covered in fancy plasterwork. It smells of old wood and is pretty intimidating.

I look at Clover, all ready to give a low, impressed whistle, but her eyes are fixed ahead, to where Mountie Amber is posing for her ID photo. "One second, please," she is telling the photographer. She shakes back her hair and smacks her lips together to redistribute her gloss. "Right, you can proceed . . ."

After the picture's been taken, she holds out her hand. "Obviously I'll need to approve it."

The photographer is so stunned, she passes it over without a word. Amber takes a look. "That will be fine," she says, handing it back and moving toward the registration desk, where a man looks up at her through half-moon glasses. "Name, please," he says, sounding tired and bored.

"Amber Horsefell."

"Subjects?"

"English and history of art."

He ticks her off the list. "You can collect your student ID from the desk at the back wall in a few minutes."

"Thank you," Amber says primly with another flick of her hair.

"Did you hear that?" Clover hisses at me. "English and history of art. There's a Mountie in both my subjects. Help, Amy!" She clutches my arm.

At the sound of Clover's voice, Amber spins round. "I heard that." She looks Clover up and down. "Newtown High? No, not scruffy enough. Weston Park. Nah, too quirky." She narrows her eyes and then smiles. "I've got it: Saint John's. I can spot a Saint John's girl anywhere. You think you're so hip and original, but you have such burning Mountie envy, it eats you up inside, like a parasitic worm."

I wait for Clover to fight back — give Amber a good tongue lashing — but she's gone mute. I'll have to say something instead.

"Mountie envy?" I snort. "You have got to be —"

"How darling," Amber says to Clover, cutting me off. "You brought along a Mini-Me to keep you company. No friends your own age. Saddo." And with a toss of her mane, she sashays away while Clover stares down at the floor.

"You OK?" I ask her.

She nods but she's biting her lip, and I can tell she's not herself.

"Once I've registered, I have to grab some paperwork from the English department and then I'm outta here," she says quietly.

"But I thought we were going to stick around, check out a few of the stands."

"Changed my mind."

"But, Clover—"

"Just leave it, Beanie. Tell you what, while I get my ID card and collect my schedule, why don't you have a look around. I'll meet you over by that funny-looking brass thing in ten minutes, OK?" She points toward the far end of the square.

"Clover, that's a very valuable Henry Moore sculpture! And it's bronze, not brass."

She shakes her head, smiling. "You're such a culture vulture, Beanie. See you in a mo'."

As she heads away, I walk back outside into the thick of the crowd, picking my way down the stands. Everyone seems to be shouting.

"Join the Sailing Club," a cute blond boy yells in my ear, nearly deafening me.

"Free foot massage at the Yoga Club," a girl in a fluffy bumblebee scarf bellows, making me jump.

I walk back, away from the stands to get a bit of space and so I can read the banners above the tables: Hockey. Chess. Yoga. Scuba Diving. Judo. Photography. Science Fiction. Comedy. *An Cumann Gaelach*. Juggling. Juggling?

The whole cobbled square is buzzing, and I'm so disappointed Clover isn't in the mood to hang out. Then I spot what looks like the college magazine stand, complete with an old-fashioned black typewriter sitting proudly on one of its many tables. The stand is covered in pink flags, each one has *Trinity Tatler* printed on it in thick black cursive script. Some of the students manning it are wearing pink fitted polo shirts, also emblazoned with the words *Trinity Tatler*.

I'm half walking away — no point in talking to them without Clover — when a singsong Galway accent mocks, "Don't join *Trinity Tatler*, then. See if I care."

A gorgeous black guy with melty chocolate eyes and a sky-high quiff of hair is talking to me. He's certainly not wearing anything resembling a pink polo shirt. He looks Odd McOdd in his checked shirt, baggy shorts, shiny blue high-tops, and geeky glasses, but *très* cute. He's perched on the edge of a table, and from the length of his amazingly strong-looking legs, he must be at least six feet tall.

"That's right," he is saying. "Walk away. We don't want any riffraff. And D4s are banned. Quite enough of them perching on the mag's desks and filing their talons already." He sweeps his eyes left and right at the girls behind the desk, and then looks directly at me. "You a D4, doll face? Nah, you don't have that pinched I'm-on-a-permanent-diet expression. And you're looking far too funky. This is your lucky day. I might just let you join our band of merry men."

I grin at him. "Sorry, but I'm not a student here. I'm just passing through."

He winks. "I get it: spying for a rival college mag. Clever. Well, you won't get a peep from these babies." He pinches his lips closed.

I laugh. "I'm only thirteen. I'm still in school."

"I never like to judge, doll face." He smiles such a cute smile that my knees nearly buckle under me. "I'm Patrick Akinjobi. Paddy to my friends. Assistant editor and general gofer. And what are you doing here today if you're not spying?"

"I'm with my aunt. She's registering today. First-year English."

"Mature student?"

I smile. "Very immature." Then something occurs to me. Paddy seems really cool — Clover would love him, and if she got involved with the magazine, maybe college wouldn't seem so daunting.

"She's only seventeen," I tell him, "but she's already a very experienced journalist. She's been working for the *Goss* during her gap year."

Paddy looks impressed. "The teen mag? It's always winning print and media awards. I've read some of their articles online."

"Clover's their agony aunt, and she also writes features," I say, encouraged by his interest. "She interviewed Matt Munroe last summer."

"Hey, I think I read that piece. The Hollywood actor with Irish roots? Exclusive interview, wasn't it?"

I nod proudly.

"This Clover sounds like my kind of gal. The mag could sure do with some experienced journos. The current crop of writers are muppets. When can I meet her?"

"Right now." And I jab a quick text to Clover.

"So what's your name?" Paddy asks.

I'm opening my mouth to tell him when a girl

appears beside him. She's another mink-haired D4 and is wearing the pink *Trinity Tatler* polo shirt with denim shorts. She has orange legs up to her armpits and a face thick with makeup. And for some reason she looks familiar.

"Hey, Paddy," she says, completely ignoring me. "My laptop's acting up again. Can you, like, fix it?" She thrusts a pearly pink laptop into his hands and then sits down on the desk with her back to me. How rude!

"Sorry," he says to me, putting the laptop down on the table and scowling at it. "Our editor's very impatient. All hail our leader." He puts both his hands in the air and pretends to kowtow.

"Just get on with it, please, Wimpy Kid," the D4 snaps. "And stop with the moaning. I bet you've done nothing except chat with people all morning. Have you even signed up any new meat? And, like, someone who can spell would be a bonus. Amber's grammar isn't great, and she types like a snail."

"So do you," he points out.

She gives a laugh. "I think you'll find writing's my thing, not typing. That's why we have minions."

Paddy turns to me again, an amused look on his face. "Feel like dropping out of school to become a copy slave? Sorry, I didn't catch your name."

"Amy," I say. "Amy Green."

The D4 whips around and looks directly at me for the first time. My jaw drops. The hair's utterly different, the goth makeup has been replaced with thick orange goo, and the accent has morphed into a mid-Atlantic drawl, but I'd recognize those piercing ice-blue eyes anywhere. *Pógarooney!* It's Cliona Bang.

Cliona has only gone and reinvented herself as a D4. Horrifying! I have to warn Clover, but I'm rooted to the spot.

Cliona narrows her eyes suspiciously. "What are *you* doing here?"

"I'm with Clover," I say, trying not to sound intimidated, even though I am. "You remember Clover, don't you?"

Something flickers over Cliona's face — worry, panic? It's hard to tell. But within nanoseconds the frown is back. "So Clover's finally decided to give college a try." She raises her perfectly plucked eyebrows. "Wonder how long she'll last."

Paddy is looking at me with interest. "How do you know our esteemed leader, then, Amy?" he asks.

"Cliona used to be a friend of my aunt's," I explain. "When she was still a goth."

Cliona squeals. "I was never a goth."

I stare at her. "You refused to leave the house without black fingernails and lips."

"That's just not true."

Paddy grins. "Reinventing your past, Cliona? I like it. You have far more depth than I'd given you credit for."

"And you used to wear black lace gloves and thick white—" I continue.

"Amy!" Cliona says strongly. "Stop or I'll—"

"Or you'll what?" Clover appears behind me. She's pale and her hands are shaking. I pray Cliona doesn't notice.

There's a loaded silence.

"So the college dropout is back," Cliona says eventually.

Clover pulls herself up straighter. "I took a gap year, Cliona. It's hardly unheard of."

"She's been writing for the *Goss,*" I say protectively.

Cliona's face is a study in unimpressed. "The magazine for tweenies?"

Paddy coughs. "Cliona? Can I just say something? Obviously you two know each other from before, but we could use a decent writer on the mag, and it sounds like Clover's got all the right credentials.

How about forgetting the past and letting Clover join the team as our new features writer? I'm Paddy, by the way, assistant editor." He gives Clover a lopsided grin.

"I'm afraid the features position has already been allocated, Paddy," Cliona says quickly, blinking a couple of times.

"Since when?" he asks.

"Since a few minutes ago," she says. "I've just appointed Amber Horsefell."

"But —" Paddy says.

Cliona puts her hand up to stop him. "I've made up my mind. Sorry, Paddy. She's perfect for the job."

Cliona turns to Clover. "I'm afraid all the slots on the mag are taken this year. And now I have to run. I'm meeting *Kendall* for lunch." She gives Clover a smug smile, and for a split second I want to punch her.

Clover looks like she's about to faint.

Don't crumble, I plead under my breath. *Stand your ground, Clover.*

But instead of saying anything, Clover staggers sideways. I grab her arm and right her. I have to get her out of there, and quickly.

"Apologies, Cliona," I say. "We're in a rush too. We're meeting Clover's boyfriend, and we're already late. He's in a band. The Golden Lions. You've probably heard of them. They're the next big thing."

Cliona looks at Clover again. Her eyes are hard to read, but there is some sort of emotion flickering behind them. "Must dash," is all she says. And then she tinkles her fingers at us and leaves in a waft of musky perfume and hairspray.

"I'm so sorry," Paddy says as soon as she's gone. He looks genuinely upset. "I had no idea she'd given Amber that slot. It's such a shame. The magazine needs a good shake-up. Cliona's running it into the ground. She's a good writer when she wants to be, but she always plays it safe. There's nothing about music or design or cutting-edge street fashion. It's all university balls and parties. And don't get me started on the website! She just won't listen to anyone else's opinion. I really hope things get better soon. Here." He hands Clover a smart gray and white business card, and she puts it in her pocket absently.

"Please stay in touch," he says. "I'm sure Cliona will change her mind. The magazine needs someone like you."

"She will," I say, adding, "sorry, Clover hasn't seen Cliona for a long time, I think she got a bit of a fright."

"I understand," he says kindly. "Sounds like Cliona's changed a lot."

"Every day," Clover says softly on the DART home. "I'm going to have to face that witch every single day. And what about *him*? I thought I was over him, Beanie. I'm such a mess."

"Forget about Cliona," I say. "And Kendall. They're not worth it."

Poor Clover. She's nervous enough about college without this horror hanging over her head.

She nods and then stares out of the window, her eyes glazed, her mind miles away. I could kill Cliona Bang. Clover's college career is at stake. I wish there was something I could do. But what?

♥ Chapter 11

"Seth, are you all right? You've been very quiet all day." I nudge him gently with my shoulder. It's lunchtime on Tuesday, and we're walking toward the pitch — but mentally he's miles away. Bailey is standing by the wall on the far side of the rugby fields with Annabelle and a gang of D4s and Crombies.

"It's Bailey," Seth says, nodding in his direction. "I tried talking to him about Mills earlier, but he just shut me down. Said he didn't want to discuss it. They were all over each other in Dundrum. I can't believe he did that to her on Friday night. And with Annabelle Hamilton. I thought he hated the D4s — but look at him now, fawning over them. I don't get it. It's all so weird."

"I know. It doesn't make sense." I think back to how he was when I confronted him at the gig. I can still see his eyes now, days later: hurt, dark, afraid. I shake my head. "I just get the feeling there's something going on with Bailey — something we don't know about. Have you met his family?"

"No. But I've been to his house in Bray. It's pretty nice, mega kitchen, loads of steel, and this really cool oven thing. He calls his old man "Mac." He's a chef. Bailey says the joke is he rarely cooks at home. Said they'd both starve if it wasn't for the local takeout."

"And his mum?"

"Didn't mention her. She certainly wasn't in the house."

"Did you not ask him where she was?"

"We're not all as nosy as you are, Amy. And we were more interested in playing Xbox than in talking about our female parentals."

I shake my head. Boys really are clueless sometimes. How can you find out about people if you don't ask questions?

"I don't think he's interested in being friends with me anymore," Seth adds glumly. "And after what he did to Mills — But do you know something weird? Polly spotted him on Killiney Beach on Saturday afternoon. He was teaching a bunch of kids to surf."

"Really? Kids? Are we talking about the same Bailey? And he's never said anything about surfing."

Seth shrugs. "I know. Strange, isn't it? Polly was surprised to find him there, all right. She hung around for a while and watched them bodyboarding. Said Bailey looked really happy just messing about in the water with the kids. He saw her and waved. He's been at our place a few times, and they got on pretty well."

I smile. "Your mum's easy to talk to. Did they talk? On the beach, I mean."

"No. He stayed in the water."

"It's just so odd. Bailey's —"

He cuts me off. "Let's talk about something else, Amy, OK? I don't really care about Bailey Otis." But I can tell from the look in his eyes that he does care — a lot. Seth's eyes don't lie. I know he feels hurt and let down. Seth doesn't make friends easily — he can be quiet and shy with people he doesn't know. It's all such a shame.

Mills is miserable too — which is understandable. First thing this morning, Annabelle told almost everyone about her "special" Golden Lions date with Bailey. So I made sure Nina Big-Mouth Pickering knew all about Mills's starring stage role.

Nina was astounded. "Are we talking about the

same Mills? Miss Goody Two-shoes? On stage at a Golden Lions gig? No way!"

I showed her the photos and video clip I'd taken on my iPhone as evidence.

"Unbelievable," she said. "Annabelle didn't mention anything about that! She claims Mills saw them smooching in their box and was devastated at being dumped. But Mills hardly looks heartbroken here . . . Wait till I tell everyone that Annabelle's lying through her teeth. Mills so obviously dumped *him*." (Nina and Annabelle have a well documented love-hate relationship.)

I smiled to myself as Nina ran off to deliver her breaking news. D4s are so easily duped.

After school a girl in my class called Lucinda Carvery comes up to me and asks, "You looking for Mills? She's in the top loo. She seems pretty upset."

"Thanks, Lucinda," I say, dashing up the corridor.

I shoulder open the door of the loos and call, "Mills? Mills?"

Nothing.

One of the cubicles is locked, and I press my ear against the wood.

"Mills? It's me, Amy."

There's a loud sniff from inside.

"Come on, Mills, open up. Don't make me crawl under the door."

There's no answer, so I get down on my hands and knees and twist my head sideways. I can see Mills's scuffed ballet flats and sensible navy socks. "Mills," I say again. "Open up, please. I'm not a circus contortionist — my neck is killing me." Straightening up, I hit my head on the bottom of the door. "Ow!" I rub the lump.

Mills clicks the latch, and the door swings back. I look at her. Her eyes are ringed with blotchy red circles, and her face is pale apart from a throbbing red nose. She's rubbing at her eyes with a piece of balled-up toilet paper. She looks terrible.

Squeezing into the cubicle beside her, I put my arm around her shoulders. "He's not worth it, Mills, honestly."

"I feel so stupid," she wails. "I don't understand what I've done. It doesn't make any sense. I can't believe he's hanging out with the D4s now. I'm so ashamed — being dumped for Annabelle! I bet everyone's laughing at me." She gives a raggedy sob and dabs her nose with the toilet paper. "I thought he liked me, Amy. I thought he really liked me."

"I know, hon, so did I. I'm so sorry. But you don't need to worry about what people think. The story is that *you* broke up with *him*, right before your Golden Lions debut. OK? I have Nina convinced, and hopefully Bailey will keep his mouth shut. And no one believes a word Annabelle says about her love life anymore." Luckily for Mills, Miss Hamilton is prone to exaggeration. There isn't a movie star in the land Annabelle hasn't "kissed" at a film premiere.

I brush her hair off her face and smile gently. "Really, Big-Mouth Nina is bound to tell the whole school, so you have nothing to worry about there."

"Thanks, Amy," she says, smiling through her tears. "But I miss him soooo much."

I hold her as she sobs her little heart out. God, I could kill Bailey Otis.

♥ Chapter 12

"Do you have any idea how many calories are in a tub of this stuff?" Clover holds up the Ben & Jerry's carton and starts scanning the side. She's dropped by so we can go through a *Goss* letter together. The house is empty apart from us. I can't remember the last time I walked into a quiet, empty house after school. It's blissful. No Mum to quiz me about homework or poke in my bag to see if I've eaten my sandwich, and no rug rats pulling at my skirt or slapping sticky hands on my skin. Score! After the day I've had, with both Seth and Mills wiped out by the Bailey virus, I deserve it.

I put my hand over the list of ingredients. "I don't want to know, Clover. Anyway, you're always telling me that dieting is pointless."

"You're right." And dipping her spoon in again, she starts shoveling ice cream down her throat like there's no tomorrow. "I don't know what's wrong with me, Beanie," she says between mouthfuls. "One minute I have no appetite at all, and the next I'm ravenous. My energy levels are all over the place."

"I'm not surprised if you're not eating properly. Did you have any lunch?"

She thinks for a second. "Actually, no."

"Right, read me this letter while I make you a toasted sandwich."

"I'm not really hungry, Beanie. And I feel a bit sick from all that ice cream."

"You're having a toastie and that's that."

"Fine. You get more and more like your mother every day."

I ignore her and start slicing cheese.

"I guess it's all the walking," she says after a few minutes. "And you can't eat in the Dead Zoo."

I stop slicing and look at her blankly.

"I've been strolling around Saint Stephen's Green Park at lunchtime," she admits. "Or visiting the Dead Zoo. I tried the National Gallery, but that was snoozeville. I really don't understand what you see in galleries, Beanie. Stuffed animals are far more interesting."

I'm about to ask why she hasn't been eating lunch at college when it dawns on me — she's afraid of bumping into Cliona or Kendall.

"You have to eat, Clover. You'll get sick."

She nods glumly. "I know."

I decide not to press her. Right now, she could do without a lecture. "So what about this letter, then?" I ask instead.

She delves through her bag — a leopard-skin Mulberry satchel, the *Goss* fashion cupboard strikes again — and pulls out a folder. "This poor soul sounds in an awful state."

I get back to sandwich making while she reads the letter to me.

Dear Clover and Amy,

You are probably going to think this is the weirdest, saddest letter that has ever landed on your desk. I have a problem. A BIG problem.

I live in Greystones with my mum. She's a flight attendant, and because she's away a lot of the time, I've been at boarding school — Rathmore Abbey. But here's the thing: Tuesday's my last day.

Mum has just come off the transatlantic flights. She's shifting to the European routes instead — so I don't have to board anymore. She says she needs to get her life back. I think she'd actually like to meet someone, someone who isn't a married pilot.

She's had a rotten time with men. There was this one guy, Dermott, who had a wife and a baby at home. Mum was devastated when he finally told her. And he only came clean because Mum invited him to spend Christmas with us and couldn't understand why he claimed he was tied up on Christmas Day.

Anyway, Mum has found me a place in Lakelands Secondary School in Bray, starting next week — a week! I'm TERRIFIED, girls, utterly heart-thumpingly petrified.

I have three days to get ready — buy the uniform, check what extra books I need — but I know nothing can prepare me for the biggest difference of all . . . You see Rathmore is all girls, and Lakelands is mixed. Please don't laugh — but I've never really spoken to a boy my own age before, not properly. I have no brothers, no cousins, no male neighbors, nothing. My life is a boy wasteland.

All my friends are girls, and I never meet any boys. If I walk into a shop and there's a guy behind the counter, I blush and stammer. It's so embarrassing — I'm sure they think I'm some sort of freak. I can't go into Xtravision anymore 'cause I get so tongue-tied — there are loads of cute boys working in there. I have to send Mum in now to get movies for me.

I really don't know what to do. I've tried talking to Mum about it, but she says that in time I'll get used to sitting beside boys every day. But I even blushed when she said this — I had no idea I'd have to sit beside them! Don't all the girls sit together? If I have to sit beside a boy, I really am doomed.

Please help! I'm seriously freaking out here!!!

Eloise Oliphant, 13

By this stage the toasted sandwich is cooking away, so I prop my bum against the kitchen counter and look down at Clover and shake my head. "I see what you mean. Poor Eloise. And Lakelands is full of D4s and Crombies. Once they realize why Eloise is blushing all the time, they'll eat her alive. What do we tell her? To spend the next week trying to buck up the courage to talk to the boys in the DVD shop?"

Clover is smiling rather smugly. "Remember back in the spring when I first took over this agony-aunt job?"

"Yes," I say cautiously. I think I know what's coming.

"I swore we wouldn't just be the usual letter-writing agony aunts, that when the time was right, we'd take action, in person. Well, Beanie, this is one of those times." She pauses as her eyes meet mine. "I need to borrow your boyfriend. Eloise needs total boy immersion, and she needs it fast. Seth's going to be one of our crash-test dummies. That coolio with you?"

I shrug. "I guess. As long as he doesn't have to kiss her."

"Course not, babes. Don't you worry. Bailey's out, obviously, creep features that he is. Shame, he's very good-looking. No news there, I suppose?"

"No, he's still hanging out with Annabelle. Mills is in bits."

"Poor moo. Tell her I was asking about her. And if she wants some revenge tactics, tell her to give me a ring. What other boys could I ask at short notice? Who's ultra hot?" She taps her lips with her finger. Suddenly her eyes light up. "I've got it. Felix!"

I snort. "There's no way Eloise will cope with a rock god. She can't even talk to spotty DVD-shop boys."

"Exactly, Beanie. Now, let's e-mail Eloise and set everything up. The sooner the better. Operation Boy Immersion is go, go, go!"

♥ Chapter 13

The doorbell rings at three o'clock the following afternoon. It's a clear, sunny day, and Mum has taken Evie to Cabinteely Park—which is perfect since Eloise is coming over for Operation Boy Immersion. I open the door and smile at the girl standing on the doorstep, twisting her hands nervously. She's stunning, with black hair swept back off her oval face by a sparkling silver hairband. She's wearing red jeans and cute silver pixie boots. Her pretty brown almond eyes fix on mine. "A-A-my?" she stammers.

I nod and smile warmly. "You must be Eloise. Come in. You found the house OK?"

She nods wordlessly. I walk into the hall, but she doesn't follow me. Instead she stays on the step and peers inside suspiciously.

"Worried we're going to kidnap you?" I joke—but from the look on her face and the way she's blushing, it's clear that this is exactly what she thinks—or worse. I feel sorry for her. I'd be nervous of walking into a stranger's house, too, especially under such weird conditions. "Clover," I call into the living room. "Come and say hi to Eloise."

Clover bounds out into the hall, grinning. "Hey there, Eloise. You're right on time. Everything's set. No need to be afraid. None of them bite."

"Them?" Eloise asks, her voice quivering a little.

Clover just smiles and touches her nose. "All will be revealed, Grasshopper. So, are you coming in or what? Mush, husky."

Eloise sighs. "I'm not sure this is such a good—"

Clover takes her arm. "Lesson one: You have to get over those nerves, Eloise. They'll gobble you up otherwise, and you'll end up like one of those saddo girls you read about sometimes who can't leave their own house." Clover pulls her gently into the hall.

Eloise looks around, clearly relieved to find that it all looks fairly normal. She takes a deep breath. "OK, what now?"

Clover points at the living-room door. "Pep talk with fellow teen Amy. Then I'll bring in our first volunteer from the holding pen, aka the kitchen. They're all a bit restless at the moment, so I'm feeding them sausage sandwiches. The more boys you meet today, Eloise, the easier you'll find it at your new school."

The instant Clover says the word "boy," Eloise's face flares up, her cheeks turning beetroot.

"Looks like we have our work cut out." Clover sighs and pats Eloise's arm. "Don't you worry, babes. We'll get you sorted for Lakelands. When's D-Day again?"

"Monday, unfortunately," Eloise says. "And I do hope this helps. Otherwise I probably will become agoraphobic—you know, afraid of going outside."

I lead her into the living room while Clover goes back into the kitchen to check on the boys. Flopping down on the sofa, I pat the seat beside me. Eloise sits, clutching her hands in her lap.

"Tell me about your mum's job," I say. "She's a flight attendant, isn't she? Sounds really interesting." (If Eloise is nervous, I figure it's best to start with something easy.)

She smiles. "It is kind of cool. She gets really cheap flights, and during the school holidays, we go to all kinds of places. She's a nut for the sun, so recently we've been to Waikiki and Phi Phi — although to be honest, I'm more of a city girl myself. We did Milan at Easter, and Budapest is the next city on our list."

"My best friend's sister lives there," I say. "She's in the Budapest Ballet Company."

"Really? Now, that is cool. It's supposed to be a really beautiful city. I can't wait to visit."

"Where else have you been?"

She shrugs. "Loads of places. San Francisco, New York, Paris, Rome. The Caribbean. And masses of beach resorts."

I whistle. "You're so lucky. And I bet all the girls in your new school will be really impressed. You must have loads of great travel stories to tell."

"I suppose I do," she says happily, and then her face drops. "But what about boys? Are they interested in travel?"

"Of course they are. Most boys are obsessed with New York. Boys are just people, Eloise — nothing more and nothing less. They're not a different species, and most of the time they're just as nervous and self-conscious as we are. But be warned, in Lakelands, in addition to boys, you'll encounter some pretty serious cliques — ones that have been honed by years of shoving students into boxes and making them stay there."

"Cliques?" Eloise shifts around on the sofa. "You mean like gangs?"

"*Exactement.* Rathmore doesn't have cliques?"

"Not really. It's a very small school. There are sporty girls, all right. But that's about it."

"No mean girls?"

She shakes her head. "No. The nuns wouldn't tolerate it."

I whistle. "Eloise, I think Lakelands is going to be a bit of a culture shock. But it's nothing you can't deal with. And if you know how to spot the cliques you're at an advantage. First of all, there are the D4s, aka the mean girls. Look out for girls who"— I put on my best D4 voice — "like, talk like they're from California and, like, begin every sentence with OMG." I drop the accent. "Other giveaway signs are obsessive use of fake tanner, poker-straight mink-colored hair, and skirts hiked up around their waists to make them shorter."

Eloise nods solemnly. "D4s. Got it. So I keep away from them, right?"

"Abso-doodle-lutely. Also steer clear of their male equivalents: the Crombies." I describe their characteristics — designer clothes, obsession with rugby, and thumping one another — and then I move on to the Emos, the Metal-Heads, the Library Nerds,

111 ♥

the Bloggers, and, finally, the Wimpy Kids, aka the chess and computer clubbers.

"What about normal kids, like me, who aren't anything?" Eloise asks. "I like music and sports and books, but I don't want to be defined by any of them."

"I feel exactly the same, Eloise. Luckily, there are plenty of fellow normaltons out there. It may take a while to find them, but I'm sure they'd love to be friends with you."

"Normaltons." She smiles, her twinkling eyes lighting up her whole face. "I like that. But what about my problem? You know, the boy thing." She starts to blush again.

"Hopefully after today that won't be so much of a problem," I say. "First we're going to introduce you to Alex—"

"A-a-alex?" she stammers, her face looking like it's on fire.

"Alex is blond and very cute," I continue, as she blushes deeper and deeper. "His interests are food, television, and trains."

"T-t-trains?" Her nose wrinkles a little.

I nod, smiling to myself, and ring the handbell on the coffee table. (Clover grabbed it from Gramps's house.) "Here comes boy number one."

The door opens, and Clover leads Alex in by the hand.

Eloise starts to laugh. "But he's only a baby." Her cheeks cool a little.

Alex scowls at her. "Me big boy."

"Sorry." Eloise gets to her feet and crouches down in front of him. "I hear you like trains."

Alex nods. "Thomas. Percy. Gordon. Hen-wie—" He starts listing off his favorites, and since he knows every single one of Thomas the Tank Engine's crew, this could go on for hours.

"OK, Alex," Clover says, cutting him off mid-flow. "Back into the holding pen for you, little man." She leads him out again.

"Big boy," he protests, and we all laugh.

As soon as he's gone, Eloise says, "He's hardly a boy, Amy."

"All boys were that size at one stage. You have to stop thinking of boys as mystical, *Lord of the Rings*–type creatures. They're just humans, and as mixed up and self-conscious as the rest of us."

She shrugs. "I suppose."

But from the doubtful look on her face, it's clear she needs more convincing.

I ring the bell again. "Next."

This time Gramps comes through the door, without Clover. "Hello, girls," he says.

Eloise stares at him in astonishment, her mouth hanging open.

"This is Len Wildgust," I say. "He's a very sprightly sixty-six. He also happens to be my grandpa."

"Eloise." Gramps holds out his hand. "Lovely to meet you."

Eloise shakes his hand, still saying nothing. I check out her cheeks. Red, yes, but not beetroot.

"May I sit down beside you?" Gramps asks politely. Clover has briefed him perfectly.

"Of course," Eloise says.

I move to give him my seat and sit in one of the armchairs instead.

"So what are your favorite subjects at school?" Gramps asks.

"Classics and art," Eloise says easily.

I let them chatter away for a few minutes before interrupting: "Time for Dave, Gramps."

Gramps nods. "No problem. Lovely to meet you, Eloise. You are a most charming young woman, I must say. Good luck in the new school. I'm sure you'll get on famously."

Seconds later Dave walks into the room a little reluctantly. As a nurse, he thinks our scheme is scientifically flawed. "You can't control blushing," he told me over breakfast. "Some people are just prone to it."

"Hi, girls," he says now. "I'm to sit down beside Eloise, is that right?"

"Yes," I say. "Eloise, this is my, um, stepdad, Dave." (I still stumble a little over the whole stepdad thing.) "He's thirty-two," I add. "A nurse. And a singer-songwriter. Soon to be the next big thing in kiddie rock."

Dave smiles at me. "Thanks, Amy."

Eloise nods and gulps as Dave takes a seat. She looks decidedly uncomfortable.

Dave must sense this because he smiles at her kindly. "Alex is my little fellow. Didn't throw anything at you, did he? He's going through a bit of a pitching phase."

Eloise laughs. "No, he was sweet."

"Sweet? Do you know what he did this morning—"

Dave tells Eloise about how Alex dipped his toothbrush in the toilet bowl and "painted" the floor tiles, and she seems to get more and more comfortable in his presence: unfolding her arms and leaning toward him. By the end of the story, she's laughing happily. "Alex sounds a real little character," she says.

"He is." Dave stands up. "Now it's time for Felix? That right?" He hesitates at the door and then says, "Boys don't mind blushing one little bit, you know, Eloise. It was one of the things that first attracted me to Amy's mum, in fact. It's pretty; don't try to hide it completely."

Eloise goes scarlet and presses her hands to her cheeks, but Dave just stands there smiling at her. "See. You look beautiful. It doesn't bother anyone, Eloise, truly. Amy blushes all the time. Even Clover does it, and she's hyper-confident."

"It's true," I say. "Everyone blushes. Especially me."

"Not like this they don't," Eloise says. "Look at my chest." There's a prickly looking pale pink rash dotted over the top of her chest.

"I didn't notice it until you pointed it out," Dave says. "Did you, Amy?"

I shake my head.

"Seriously?" Eloise stares down at her chest. "You can't see it?"

We both shake our heads.

She grins. "That's great. I thought it was really noticeable. That's made my day."

"And you've been having conversations quite happily with both Gramps and Dave," I point out.

"I have, haven't I?" she says. "I wonder what Felix will be like."

"Ask him about his music," Dave says kindly. "He plays the guitar. Boys like being asked about movies and telly programs too. Most of us are movie obsessed."

"Thanks for the tip," Eloise says brightly.

After Dave's left the room, I figure I'd better warn Eloise that she might find Felix a bit more of a challenge — but it's too late, he's already walking in the door.

Eloise's eyes are fixed on his face — on those piercing green eyes, with their Bambi eyelashes, and chiseled cheekbones. Strangely enough, though, she's so mesmerized, her cheeks are not as crimson as I would have expected them to be.

"Hiya, Eloise," Felix says in his lazy drawl. "Aren't you a doll." He sits on the sofa beside her, his long legs stretched out in front of him. (OK, now her face is starting to burn.) "I'm Felix, a friend of Amy's and Clover's. Charmed to meet you." He kisses her on both cheeks. She looks delighted yet mortified.

"Dave said you play the guitar," she manages to get out without stammering. "Are you in a band?"

Go, Eloise! I think. As Felix starts telling her about

the Golden Lions, she's so interested, she seems to have forgotten to be embarrassed. Plus her cheeks are cooling down.

The door opens a little then, and Clover pops her head round it. "Seth's just arrived. Wants a quick word, Amy."

"You guys OK for a second?" I ask, looking at Eloise.

"Yes!" she says. "Felix is telling me about his band and all the gigs they have lined up. Isn't it exciting?"

"No kidding. OK — see you in a mo'." I walk out of the room and close the door behind me.

Clover is in the hall with Seth, who is sitting on the bottom step of the stairs, waiting to talk to me.

"Brains and Felix have to be at RTÉ in half an hour to record 'Caroline' for a radio show," Clover says. "Do you want Eloise to meet Brains, or is Felix enough? I'd love to snatch a few minutes with Brains if you can spare him."

"Don't worry about Brains," I say. "Felix is doing brilliantly. He's being so sweet. I think Operation Boy Immersion is really helping, Clover."

She grins. "Good. We aim to please. I think she's all set for a real teenager. You ready, Seth?"

He nods and gets to his feet. "Sure."

"Coola boola. Right, I'm off to cuddle my boyfriend while he's actually in the same part of the country as me. See you later."

"So what's the deal?" Seth asks as soon as she's gone. "I just have to be nice to this Eloise girl, yeah? Get her used to boys."

"Correcto." I pause. "Seth?"

"Amy?" He looks at me, his blue eyes soft and a little serious — the whole Bailey thing is really taking its toll.

"Thanks for doing this."

He smiles gently. "If it makes my favorite girl happy . . ."

Felix looks up as we walk into the living room. "Time for me to motor, Eloise. Really cool to meet you. Listen for us on the radio."

Eloise beams. "Oh, I will. I promise. And thanks for all the advice."

"You're welcome." He kisses her cheeks again, and she blushes — but she looks less mortified.

"Hey, man," Felix says to Seth as he walks past us.

"Um, hey," Seth murmurs. He's a huge Golden Lions fan, so it's no wonder he's a bit tongue-tied.

Eloise is positively glowing as Seth sits down beside her. "Hi, Eloise," he says. "I'm Seth."

She smiles at him a little shyly, blood ebbing

in and out of her cheeks, and then manages a small "Hi."

"I'm Amy's boyfriend," he adds.

"Do you like music?" she asks him gingerly.

"Yeah," he says easily, sitting back in his chair. "I like all kinds of stuff—bit of vintage punk, bit of soul, indie, some rock, Golden Lions, of course . . ."

"And what kind of movies are you into?"

He smiles at her, his eyes sparkling. *Good question, Eloise!* Seth is a movie nut. He watches everything from slasher films to old black-and-whites. And Eloise is smiling back at him, her cheeks dusky pink, not fire-engine red. Success!

"Back in a second," I murmur happily—I want to tell Clover our plan has worked!

When I walk into the kitchen, I find Clover sitting on Brains's knee. He's stroking her hair and murmuring in her ear. Today a gold elastic hairband is cutting through his Afro, and he's wearing yellow coveralls. Ah, the usual Brains "style." Outside, Dave, Felix, Gramps, and Alex are playing football in the backyard.

"Sorry to interrupt," I say. "Can I borrow you for a moment, Clover?"

Brains looks over at me and grins. "Always

dragging her away from me, Amy Damey," he says with a fake sigh. "You be Speedy Gonzales with my girl, ya hear? Me and Felix have to shoot off in ten minutes for RTÉ, then we have a late gig in Cork this evening, and I need more sweet lovin' from my woman first."

I laugh. "I'll be quick, I promise."

He lifts Clover off his knee, then stands up and kisses the top of her head. "Missing you already, buttercup," he says before going to join the other boys in the yard.

"So what's up, Beanie?" Clover asks as soon as he's out the door.

"Operation Boy Immersion has been a total success, sir!" I say, clicking my heels together and saluting her. "Eloise and Seth are chatting away like old friends. And her flaming blush has chilled to a low glimmer. Clover, you're a genius."

"Today, Eloise; tomorrow, world domination," she says with a grin. "Beanie, our work here is done."

While Clover sees Eloise out, I walk back into the living room to catch Seth. He's standing by the window, staring out. As soon as he hears me, he turns around.

"You OK?" I ask him. "I know the whole Bailey

thing has really knocked you sideways." He's been quiet for days now, and I've been trying to find a moment to talk to him.

"I'm fine. Just—" He shrugs. "I miss hanging out with him, you know."

"I understand," I say gently, a ripple of anger running up my spine. How dare Bailey Otis squash my friends like ants under his stupid Doc Martens! I put out my arms and pull Seth so close, I can smell his lemony hair gel. Sometimes, we all need a hug.

♥ Chapter 14

Mum corners me in the hall on Sunday afternoon. "Amy, I have to nip out to the shops and Dave's at work. Can you keep an eye on the monsters? And keep them away from the kitchen. My Dictaphone and book notes are on the table."

"No problemo."

As soon as she closes the front door behind her, I have a thought: Finn's intimate details are sitting on our kitchen table, just crying out to be investigated. I just need some time!

I dash toward the door and swing it open. Mum is already backing the car out of the drive, but I call out to her and she buzzes down her window. "Everything OK, Amy?"

"Mum, I'm not doing anything today. Why don't you go to Dundrum? Have a look around the shops. You're always complaining that you don't get a minute to yourself."

Mum looks at me suspiciously. "Are you after something, Amy? New Ugg boots, is that it?"

"Nah, I've gone off them. I just thought you could do with some time out. You look tired."

Mum presses the skin under her eyes with the tips of her fingers. "Do I?" She sighs. "I guess with the kids and all this Finn stuff . . . Anyway, thank you, Amy — that would be a real treat. I won't be longer than a couple of hours. Are you sure you can cope?"

I beam at her. "Positive."

After settling Alex and Evie in the living room with cookies and *Peppa Pig*, I sit down at the kitchen table, feeling strangely nervous. I know I shouldn't be reading Mum's notes, but it's all going to be published soon for the whole world to read, so surely it can't do any harm?

Mum's yellow notebook, Dictaphone, and a large manila envelope are on the table. I pick up the notebook and turn to the first page. "*Pot Luck* Outline," I read in Mum's curly handwriting.

<u>Chapter 1: Introduction to Finn's current career</u>
The adoring fans, the telly show, the cookbooks — but how did he get here?

<u>Chapter 2: Finn's early years in Portstewart</u>
Leaving school and going to work in the Ice House Restaurant, where he met his first love, Lane Otis.

I read it again. Does that really say Lane *Otis*, like Bailey Otis? I peer at Mum's handwriting. It does. What a spooky coincidence. There can't be that many people in Ireland called Otis.

Chapters 3 to 6 are all about Finn's career in London and his rise from kitchen dishwasher to Michelin-starred chef. I scan down the page.

The notes end with "Chapter 7: Finn moves back to Dublin from London in July." And that's as far as Mum has gotten — or since he only moved back recently, maybe that's the end of the book. But then I spot another note scrawled in capital letters across the bottom of the page:

TALK TO FINN ABOUT THE LETTERS FROM HIS SON — COULD BE THE KEY TO THE WHOLE BOOK!

Letters from his son? Finn Hunter has a son?! Wow!

I feel so guilty finding out all this stuff about Finn that I glance around the kitchen nervously, as if someone is watching me, and my eye falls on the envelope. I know I shouldn't delve any further into Finn's private life — but it's so tempting that I can't help myself.

I tip the contents onto the table — dozens more envelopes fall out, all addressed to Finn Hunter in the same spidery handwriting. I run my fingers over a couple of them, my heart thumping in my chest, and before I know what I'm doing, I've picked one up, pulled the letter out, and started to read:

DEAR FINN,

DID YOU GET MY OTHER LETTERS? WHY HAVEN'T YOU REPLIED YET? I HOPE I GOT THE ADDRESS RIGHT.

I WISH YOU'D WRITE BACK. THINGS ARE RUBBISH HERE. JENNIE LEFT LAST WEEK. MAC'S REALLY CUT UP ABOUT IT. I MISS HER TOO. WRITING TO YOU WAS HER IDEA. IT FEELS STUPID WITHOUT HER.

WHEN CAN I COME AND SEE YOU? OR MAYBE YOU COULD COME HERE TO DUBLIN? THERE'S LOADS OF THINGS I WANT TO ASK YOU ABOUT.

MAC WON'T TALK ABOUT YOU OR MUM OR ANY OF THAT STUFF. BUT SOMETIMES I JUST WISH SOMEONE WOULD TALK ABOUT IT, YOU KNOW? GET IT

ALL OUT IN THE OPEN. IT'S LIKE THIS BIG, BLACK SECRET AND WE'RE NOT
ALLOWED TO SAY ANYTHING OR, I DON'T KNOW, THE WORLD WILL BLOW UP OR
SOMETHING.

ANYWAY, PLEASE WRITE BACK SOON!

BAILEY OTIS

I gasp and stare at the page. *Bailey*. It says Bailey Otis!
There can't be two boys called Bailey Otis in Ireland,
can there? I put down the letter and stare into space.
Mum's notes definitely said "letters from his son." Can
it be true? Can Finn Hunter really be Bailey's dad?

I pull out another letter — same handwriting, same
signature at the bottom. I check the postmark; it was
sent in November last year. I scan the letter and find
the words "This is about my tenth letter. And you still
haven't written back. Do you hate me that much?"

Sifting through the pile I find the final letter. It
was sent in April this year:

THIS IS THE LAST LETTER. I'M NEVER WRITING TO YOU AGAIN. JENNIE WAS
WRONG. SHE SAID I SHOULD GIVE YOU A CHANCE. THAT MAYBE YOU WERE SCARED
TO CONTACT ME AFTER ALL THIS TIME. AND SCARED OF WHAT MAC MIGHT DO
TO YOU.

YOU'RE NOT SCARED. YOU JUST DON'T CARE ABOUT ME. I'M YOUR BIG
MISTAKE. DON'T WORRY, YOU WON'T HEAR FROM ME AGAIN. I HATE YOU!

This time, Bailey hadn't signed his name.

I sit back in my chair, thoughts swirling. No wonder Bailey's so messed up. But why didn't Finn write back? He seems like a really decent guy.

I flick through the notebook, looking for clues — but there's nothing much in there, just some information about Finn's time in London, with restaurant names and dates. Nothing about Bailey. Then my eyes come to rest on the Dictaphone. Picking it up, I turn it over and over in my hands, and then, trying not to think about what Mum will do to me if she catches me listening to it, I press Play.

". . . And when Mum died in May, I had to go through her things, you know how it is." It's Finn's voice, and I listen carefully. *"And that's when I found all of Bailey's letters. He'd sent them to my home address in Portstewart, but Mum had never forwarded them on. I guess she thought she was protecting me . . . I don't know what was going through her mind, to be honest. She was always a world unto herself. She encouraged me to run off to London when I got Lane pregnant. I wanted to marry Lane, try to make a go of things, but Mum persuaded me against it. She said Lane was flighty, would never be happy, and that it would be no life for me with a young baby and wife to support. I deserved better."*

"And you believed her?" Mum asks him. She sounds surprised, shocked even.

"She was my mum. She was all I had. What was I supposed to do? I was only seventeen. I didn't know what to think. I had visions of Mac—that's Lane's dad and Bailey lives with him now—coming after me with a shotgun for getting Lane in trouble like that. Especially after he'd taken me into his restaurant and treated me like a son. Jennie, Lane's stepmum, tried to persuade me to stay, but I wouldn't listen."

"So you ran off to London while Lane was pregnant?" Mum asks.

Finn gives a deep sigh. "I'm not proud of it. Biggest mistake of my life."

"When did you find out that the baby had been born? That you had a son?"

"Mum rang me a week after it happened. It all seemed a bit unreal, to be honest, like it was nothing to do with me, you know. Mum said to put it out of my mind. She said Lane and the baby were going to live with Mac and Jennie—everything was already sorted. I wanted to send the baby a present, some money or something, but Mum said that was a bad idea. It would only go giving them ideas about child support. I sent twenty quid, anyway, in a blank baby card. It wasn't much, but it was all I *could afford. And then I tried to forget all about the lad until"* — he pauses — *"all that stuff in the paper about Lane abandoning him. The printout I gave you the other day . . ."* There's another long pause.

"I'm sorry," he says finally. *"I — No. I just can't. Forget I said anything. In fact, I think I've made a mistake. I should never have mentioned Bailey at all, or any of that baby business. I don't want it in the book, OK?*

"I was hoping things would be different by now. I moved back from London to try and make contact with him. To make up for the past, you know. But he won't talk to me, you see. And Mac's no help. He refuses to speak to me as well — let alone meet up. Jennie was better — sent me photos of Bailey every now and then. I found them at Mum's when I discovered the letters. I've tried writing to Mac, ringing him at work, e-mailing. Nothing.

"I was at my wit's end, so I rang the house last Friday. Bailey picked up — but it was a disaster. He went mental: started yelling through the phone, saying he hated my guts —" He breaks off, sounding upset. *"I've messed everything up. My son hates me . . . my own son. And to be honest, I don't blame him. I'll never forgive myself."*

Friday! That was the night of the Golden Lions gig. No wonder Bailey was all over the place. He felt he'd been abandoned by Mills and Finn, both on the same day.

Mum's speaking now. *"Would you have written back — if the letters had reached you?"*

"Honestly?" Finn says, blowing out his breath. *"I don't know. I like to think I would have, but back in London, it was all about me and my career. I never had time for anyone else."* He gives a dry laugh. *"No wonder I can't keep a girlfriend. I'll probably die alone too, just like Mum."*

"That's a terrible thing to say, Finn," Mum says. *"You're young."*

"I feel about a hundred. Look, I'm sorry for burdening you with all this, Sylvie. Just what you don't need, right?"

"It's my job, remember? I'm writing your story. But I think we should include the baby story. Maybe without mentioning your son's name or anything to do with the newspaper reports. Why don't you use the book as a way of reaching out to him? Send a copy to him, see if he responds. It's worth a try. Admit you've made a lot of mistakes and say that you want to make it up to him. You could write an open letter to your son in the book, Finn, for the whole world to see."

"Do you think it would work?" Finn's voice sounds achingly hopeful. *"I'd give anything to meet Bailey, to try and put things right."*

"It's worth a try," Mum says softly. Then there's a click and the tape ends.

I sit at the table for ages, staring into space. Poor Bailey. No one should have to deal with being rejected by both their mum and their dad — and in Bailey's mind, Finn rejected him twice: first at birth and then when he never replied to his letters. I imagine Bailey sitting at his own kitchen table, writing letter after letter to his father, and never hearing anything back. No wonder he's so unhappy and confused.

I sit there a few minutes longer before starting to shuffle Mum's notes back into place, in case she comes home unexpectedly early. As I pick up Mum's yellow notebook, a folded sheet of paper falls out of the back of it. I open it up. It's a printout of a newspaper article.

DUBLIN TODDLER ABANDONED

A toddler, 3, was discovered abandoned in a house in Dublin over the weekend. Social services have confirmed that the child was found in a distressed state and had been on his own for some time.

The boy, referred to as Baby X because he cannot be named for legal reasons . . .

I stop, tears filling my eyes. I just can't read on — it's too horrible. Suddenly there's a knock on the front door. I hurriedly shove the sheet back into the notebook, in case it's Mum and she's forgotten her door key again, but then I hear Clover calling through the mail slot: "I know you're in there, Beanie. Open up."

Relieved, I swing open the door.

"What's wrong?" she asks, spotting my teary eyes. "Is it Seth? Did you guys have a fight?"

"No! It's Bailey," I say, tears rolling down my cheeks. "I think I know why he's so messed up, Clover."

♥ Chapter 15

"Let me get this right," Clover says slowly when I've stopped talking. "Bailey Otis, the guy who broke Mills's heart, is Finn Hunter's son? Are you positive?"

I give a huge nod. "Yes!"

She whistles. "This is explosive stuff, Beanie. And as for the letters Bailey sent Finn, any journalist would have a field day with that information. I can see the headlines now" — she frames her hands in the air — "'TOP CHEF REJECTS LONG-LOST SON SHOCKER.'"

I look at her, aghast. "You wouldn't, Clover."

"'Course not, Beanie. My lips are sealed. No wonder Bailey can't hold down a relationship with someone like Mills, though."

"What do you mean?"

"Mills treated him like a prince, right? So he pushed her away and took up with Annabelle Hamilton — who probably treats him like dirt. He doesn't believe he deserves someone kind and decent like Mills — or maybe he's just afraid of getting too close and getting hurt again, like he was when he wrote to Finn and never got a reply."

"You should be doing psychology, Clover. How come you have such people smarts?"

"Experience, babes. School of hard knocks. I was an orphan, I was." She starts singing "It's a Hard-Knock Life" in a Little Orphan Annie voice. Then, going serious again, she says, "It's terrible for Bailey and everything, but I don't see why you're so upset, babes."

"There's something else, Clover. About Bailey." And I fetch the article from the back of Mum's notebook and rejoin Clover in the living room.

"You have to read this," I say and, while she does so, I check on Evie, who's still transfixed by the talking pigs on TV. I crouch down on the floor and play with Alex, whizzing one of his trains up and down his wooden track and making "choo-choo" noises. For some reason, it makes me feel a little better. I lean over and kiss the top of his head, which smells a bit sweaty — he hates having his hair washed. Then I glance up at Clover. She's sitting dead still, staring at me.

"Beanie," she says gently. "How much did you read? And what's this got to do with anything?"

"Only a few lines — but I also listened to some of Mum's interviews with Finn on her Dictaphone. I think Bailey is Baby X."

"*Bailey?* Are you sure?"

"Pretty much. I wish he wasn't, Clover, believe me, but it all fits. I would have to read the whole newspaper article to be absolutely certain, though. Will you stay here while I do?"

She shakes her head, her eyes sad. "Beanie, trust me. You don't need to know all the details. I'm begging you. Leave it be."

"Bailey's my friend. I have to know what happened to him. And you're here now."

"Yes, I am. I'll stay for as long as you like and entertain the tiddlers while you read. I think I need a sticky hug from Alex and Evie. Here." She hands me the article, and I perch on the side of the armchair and pick up where I'd left off:

The boy, referred to as Baby X because he cannot be named for legal reasons, was severely dehydrated when discovered by neighbors Mary and Alf Cosgrove on Monday morning.

His mother had pushed a note under their door, but it wasn't discovered until Monday since they had been unexpectedly called away for the weekend to visit a sick relative. In the note the mother had said that she regretted leaving the child but would not be back. She instructed the couple to contact the baby's grandfather in Portstewart, County Antrim.

The boy was taken to Temple Street Children's Hospital and is thought to be making a swift recovery.

His grandfather has been contacted.

When I've finished, Clover lifts her head from the train track where she's playing with Alex. "You OK, Beanie?"

"Yeah. Just want to see if there's any more info on the Internet."

Switching on the computer, I Google "Baby X." There are dozens of results: "THE BISCUIT BOY" (*Irish Daily Express*), "THE MIRACLE OF BABY X" (*Irish Sun*), "DUBLIN'S HOME ALONE CHILD" (*Irish Independent*), "LITANY OF QUESTIONS OVER ABANDONED CHILD" (*Irish Times*).

I read through each article carefully, but they all say pretty much the same thing. Now I'm convinced — it's Bailey, all right. When I've finally finished reading, I look up from the screen, wipe away my tears, and take a few deep breaths. "It's definitely Bailey, Clover. It all fits."

"I'm so sorry, Beanie," Clover says from the sofa — she's hugging Evie on her knee. "Some people don't deserve to have children. I don't know what to say. It's honestly one of the saddest things I've ever read. And I can't believe the baby — Baby X — is your friend Bailey. It's so surreal. How can a mother do something like that? To her own son?"

A huge lump forms in my throat. "I know."

"Come here, Beanie" — Clover throws her arms open — "group girlie hug with Evie."

I sit down on the sofa, and she puts her arm around my shoulder and pulls me close. I shut my eyes, willing my tears to stop, and for a while time seems to stand still.

Then I hear Alex say, "Me hug," before feeling his little body piling on top of us. I open my eyes just in time to see him crawl onto Clover's lap and throw himself toward me in a dangerous toddler lunge.

"Alex, you've just elbowed me in the stomach,

you troll," I say. And despite everything, Clover and I start laughing.

We're still sitting on the sofa — Evie asleep on Clover's knee, me and Alex curled around Clover like newborn puppies — watching *Peppa Pig*, when Mum walks in, swinging a shopping bag. She smiles. "You lot look cozy."

"Ma-ma," Alex says, jumping up and holding out his arms. "Ma-ma."

She drops the bag and swings him around, then rests him on her hip.

"What did you buy, sis?" Clover asks, eyeing the bag. "Give us a peek."

Mum bends down — Alex's weight and kicking legs making it rather awkward — and pulls out what looks like Batman's cape.

Clover bites her lip — Mum's shopping mistakes are legendary. Mum puts Alex down on the floor and throws the material over her head. For a second she's lost in the swathes of black cloth, but then her head pops through the hole. "It's a poncho," she says with a grin. "They're all the rage apparently, and I needed a new coat. What do you think?"

"Doesn't do much for your curves," Clover says diplomatically.

"Amy?" Mum asks hopefully. "Do you like it?"

I make a face. "Sorry, Mum. It might be useful if you want to dress up for Halloween, though. Add a pointy hat and, *voilà*, one witch costume."

Mum pulls it back over her head, making her hair go all sticky-up from the static, and stuffs it quickly back into the bag. "I'll take it back."

"Probably best," Clover says kindly. "If you're looking for a coat, Sylvie, try Zara. They have fab army-style ones that nip in at the waist and would really suit you."

"Thanks, Clover," Mum says. "And I might take you or Amy with me next time. You girls have such good fashion eyes." She flops down on the sofa beside us. "So what have you two been up to, then?"

I stare down at my hands. I've put everything back carefully on the kitchen table, but I still feel guilty.

"We were discussing our plans for your bachelorette party," Clover jumps in, saving my bacon. "Weren't we, Amy?"

"Abso-doodle-lutely," I say firmly. "And it's all top secret, so don't even ask."

Mum looks a little worried. "As long as it doesn't involve tiaras, Temple Bar, and chocolate you-know-whats, I'll be happy." (Dublin's Temple Bar is notorious for wild bachelorette parties.)

"Temple Bar's not on the agenda," Clover says, "but chocolate willies — now there's a thought . . ."

"Clover!" Mum glares at her.

Clover laughs. "Only winding you up, sis, settle your tights."

Evie stirs a little and then opens her eyes. Within seconds she's wailing like a banshee.

"Bottle time for this little madam," Mum says, taking her off Clover. "Then I'll put her down. You guys OK with the junior kamikaze here?" She nods down at Alex, who is crashing his wooden Thomas engine into Percy at full speed.

"No problemo, Mum," I say.

As soon as she's out the door, Clover turns to me and asks in a low voice, "Has Sylvie copped that you know Finn's son?"

"Of course not," I whisper back. "I only found out myself this afternoon, remember? Should I tell her?"

Clover shrugs. "I have two minds about it. You see, Sylvie told me she's signed a confidentiality agreement with Finn's agent. She can't talk about any of the stuff Finn tells her ever — not even after the book's published. I think you reading her notes is a breach of contract."

I wince. "So she might lose her job, you mean?"

"It depends how seriously they take the agreement. I guess it all hinges on what you want to do with the information."

I look at her in surprise. "*Do*? Meaning what?"

"I know your weird little brain inside out, Bean Machine. You want to help Bailey and Finn work things out, don't you? Orchestrate some sort of father-and-son reunion."

I can't hide anything from Clover. That's exactly what's been going through my head since the moment I discovered the Bailey-Finn connection. "But how, Clover?" I ask. "Bailey won't talk to him. Finn's tried loads of times."

"But they haven't ever seen each other face-to-face, right?"

"Correct. By the sound of it, Finn's rung the house, but they've never met."

She thinks for a second and then says, "What does Bailey look like?"

"What's that got to do with anything? Besides, you've seen him — at the gig in the Olympia."

"In the distance. Bear with me for a second: does he look anything like Finn?"

I consider this. Bailey has jet-black hair; Finn's is sandy brown, but they both have piercing green eyes, stellar cheekbones, and strong, full lips you can't help but stare at.

"Come to think of it," I say, "apart from the hair, then yes, they look very alike."

"So if they were to meet in person, it would be pretty overwhelming, right? Because they look so much alike, I mean. And Finn seems like a cool guy, sincere, very likable, loads of charisma, and he seems to genuinely want to make it up to Bailey from what you've said. What if we managed to trick the two of them into the same room—would their shared chemistry kick in? Would Bailey be able to overlook the past, swallow his pride, and actually talk to Finn?"

"Engineer a meeting without telling either of them? Is that what you mean?"

"Precisely." Her eyes are twinkling. "What do you think? Would it work?"

"I have no idea, but it's got to be worth a shot."

"Good. Is there anything that links them apart from genetics? We need to hang their meeting on something."

I begin to smile. "I think I've got it. Clover, you're a genius!"

♥ *Chapter 16*

"I don't know about you, Beanie," Clover says as we crunch along Killiney Beach, "but I'm really nervous. What if Bailey refuses to speak to Finn? It's going to get us both in a whole heap of trouble."

"As long as we can keep Mum's name out of it, I don't really care, to be honest. Anyway, it can hardly make things worse, can it?"

"I suppose not." Clover sounds doubtful, though. I don't blame her. She's put herself on the line for this. She rang Finn's agent, Britta, and set up a *Goss* interview with Finn. She also promised a big photo shoot on the beach to tie in with his whole Irish Surfing Chef persona. Since it's Saturday, we're hoping Bailey will show up soon to give his usual surfing lessons.

When we reach the sand dunes to the right of the Martello Tower, Finn's already there, looking like a rock star in his battered brown leather jacket and wraparound shades. "Hi, girls." He grins. "Nice to see you again." He rubs his hands together. "So where's this photographer, then? I want to catch the rugby game later, yeah? It would be great to wrap things up quickly."

"Don't worry, I'm sure she'll be here in a jiffy," Clover says, her eyes flitting away from Finn's to study the water.

"Surf's up," Finn says, following her gaze. "Wish I had my board with me. East coast's not usually the best for surfing, but the wind's coming from the perfect direction today for some board action."

And right on cue, a couple of boys of about ten or eleven run onto the beach, surfboards under their arms. Ramming their boards into the sand near the shore, they quickly strip down, and within seconds they're racing toward the waves in sleek black wet suits.

Finn laughs. "They're keen."

Soon the water is filled with black bodies, flicking water at one another, laughing, trying to catch waves, and toppling off boards. And then the atmosphere suddenly changes: the boys stop horsing around, and one of them gestures toward a tall boy who has just appeared on the shore. He's wearing a beanie and sunglasses, but there's no mistaking who it is: Bailey.

I grab Clover's arm, just as one of the surfers yells, "Hi, Bailey, we've been waiting for you."

Bailey thrusts his board into the sand, walks toward the water's edge, black rucksack bobbing on his back, and starts chatting with them.

Finn is frozen to the spot, the color draining from his cheeks. Pulling off his sunglasses, he stares at Bailey, his eyes dark and intense. Then he looks at us. "What's going on? Who's that older lad with the board?"

"Do you recognize him?" Clover asks.

Finn's quiet for a few agonizing seconds, then eventually he says slowly, "I think so."

"His name is Bailey Otis," I say. "Would you like to meet him?" I can't keep the hopeful, excited tone out of my voice, and Finn recognizes it.

He stares at me, looking utterly confused. "Bailey? I don't understand. What's he doing here?" He looks around frantically. "Is this some kind of weird setup? Are there cameras?"

"No!" Clover says. "Of course not. We just thought you might like to talk to him, face-to-face."

"Bailey's in my class in school," I explain,

feeling sorry for Finn. I can't begin to imagine how overwhelmed he must be feeling right now. "We're friends."

"Did he tell you about me?" Finn asks, his eyes boring into mine.

Yikes! "Not exactly."

"I think you'd better spill the beans right now," Finn says, his tone serious. "The truth, please, Amy."

I gulp. He seems really angry. Whatever I was expecting, it wasn't this. I'd thought he'd be grateful, having clearly been dying to meet his son in person.

"It was me," Clover says quickly, taking the bullet. "I was digging around, doing some research before this interview. I talked to a couple of people and found out about your son. Amy's best friend was going out with a Bailey Otis, and as it's a very unusual name, I put two and two together —"

"And came up with five." Finn runs his hands through his hair. He seems very out of sorts. "And it's none of anyone's business — especially not yours."

"But it's true, isn't it?" I pipe up. "Bailey *is* your son."

I must have spoken too loudly, because at that moment Bailey swings round and stares at us. His gaze moves from me, glances over Clover, and rests directly on Finn. And he does not look happy. Their eyes lock. Bailey's left cheek is distorted; he must be chewing it savagely. For a second, his eyes are soft, almost misty — and then it's like someone has flicked a switch, and they go hard and steely.

"How dare you?" he spits out at Finn as he marches up the sand toward us. "Did you have me followed or something? And what's *she* doing here?" He glares at me.

"Bailey," Finn says, his voice quivering a little. "Bailey, please, can't we just talk?"

"NO! Not now, not ever. Stop trying to contact me. I don't want anything to do with you, understand. If I see you here again I'll . . . I'll call the cops. Have you up for harassment and sell the story to the papers. The mighty Finn Hunter stalking a teenage boy! That would look just great in the headlines."

Finn's face crumples. "It wasn't my idea. I thought I was doing a photo shoot for a magazine. These girls —"

"Are idiots," Bailey snaps. He looks at me, his eyes full of pain. "Amy Green, you're some piece of work. Who told you I come here? Polly? Seth? Are you trying to get back at me for hurting Mills, is that it?"

"What?" I say. "No! I was trying to *help*. I thought if you saw your dad in the flesh —"

"Dad?" Bailey says angrily. "The man doesn't

deserve that name. Now leave me alone, all of you. Especially you, Amy." He turns to Finn again. "And what are you still doing here?"

"Bailey, please listen —"

But before he gets a chance to finish his sentence, Bailey swings his arm and punches Finn hard, his fist impacting just above Finn's jaw.

Finn stumbles backward onto the sand, clutching his face, while Bailey runs toward the sea and shouts, "Surfing's off today, lads, sorry." Then he grabs his board and storms across the sand dunes, away from us, away from Finn — without a backward look.

"I'm so sorry," I tell Finn, who looks as shell-shocked as I feel. His lip is bleeding, and he's pressing his fingers against it to try to stem the flow. I can hear Bailey's voice in my head: "Are idiots."

Idiots . . . idiots . . . idiots.

I'm so stupid and ashamed. What was I thinking? Did I really think Bailey would yell, "Daddy, I forgive you," and run into Finn's arms like in a Disney movie? Life isn't like that.

Clover puts her arm around my shoulder. "It's OK, Beanie. It's not your fault. You were trying to help."

"But it *is* my fault. I should never have interfered. Bailey's right: I am an idiot. And he *hit* Finn."

"I'm all right," Finn says. "It looks worse than it

is." He's staring out at the boys, still playing in the waves: happily oblivious of what has just happened. "I'm the fool," he continues. "I've made a right mess of everything. I should never have run off on Lane like that. Man, it was unforgivable. I don't deserve a son." He looks at me and Clover, his eyes glistening with tears. "I know you were only trying to fix things, but there's nothing any of us can do now. We all have to respect the dude's wishes and leave him alone."

Alone? I feel a wave of sadness. Finn's right, though; it's beyond our control. And to top it all, now I'm going to have to tell Mum what I've done before Finn does. She's going to kill me!

♥ Chapter 17

I was wrong: Mum doesn't kill me.

After the Killiney Beach incident, Clover took me for hot chocolate in Mugs café in Dalkey to try to cheer me up before dropping me off at home.

"I'll tell Sylvie what happened with Finn and Bailey," she said as we drove toward the house. "It was my fault too, Beanie. You shouldn't have to take the rap alone."

So now we're sitting around the kitchen table, me, Mum, and Clover, all staring at one another. Clover has just finished telling Mum the whole story.

"Poor Bailey," Mum is saying. "He's had such a sad life. It's such a shame he won't talk to Finn. Personally, I think they both need each other."

"You're not annoyed with me for reading your notes?" I ask, surprised. I bite my lip and then, guessing it's probably best to come completely clean, add: "I listened to the tape too and read Bailey's letters to Finn."

Mum smiles gently. "Why do you think I left everything on the kitchen table, Amy? I knew you wouldn't be able to resist a little peek. And I had this really strong feeling that the boy who has been causing Mills all the grief was Finn's son. It was just too much of a coincidence otherwise."

I stare at Clover. "What have you been telling Mum?"

Clover shrugs. "Nothing, Beanie. Your secrets are my secrets. How do you know about the Mills and Bailey drama-rama, Sylvie?"

"Sue was very worried," Mum says. "Mills wasn't eating properly — or sleeping. So Sue had a little chat with her and found out about Bailey Otis. She asked my advice as to how to help her, mum to mum. After that, I put two and two together. There can't be many boys with that name in Dublin."

"Mills's mum was asking you for advice?" Clover asks. Clover and I both give a laugh at the same time.

"What?" Mum demands. "I give great advice!"

"That's right, Sylvie," Clover says, her lips curling into a smile. "You keep telling yourself that."

"So let's get this straight, Mum," I say. "You left the stuff on the table knowing you couldn't say anything to me directly?"

"Exactly. I felt I had to do something. Get them together somehow. I couldn't come up with anything, so I thought of you, Amy. You're always so good at fixing things. Of course, it doesn't always go as planned, does it, pet? Sometimes, like today, it's a complete disaster. But at least you try."

"I think that's what they call damning with faint praise," Clover says. "I thought you took a gobbledygook parenting course once, Sylvie. Maybe you should think about going back."

Mum scowls at her. "I have exemplary parenting skills, thank you very much. And when you have your own family, you'll realize just how difficult raising children is, Miss High-and-Mighty."

I put up my hands to interrupt them. "Hello? Why are you two fighting? Calm down, people. We have other things to worry about at the moment." Suddenly something occurs to me. "Mum, Bailey lives with his grandpa, Mac. Does Finn talk about him much?"

"All the time. Mac Otis was like a father to him.

Finn feels he really let him down, getting his daughter pregnant and then running off like that. Why do you ask?"

"I was just wondering . . . It's nothing important."

The front door bangs, and a moment later Alex comes dashing into the room, followed by Dave, who is carrying Evie in his arms.

"There goes the peace and quiet," Mum says, standing up. "Alex, why are you so wet?"

"He's been jumping in puddles," Dave says.

"But he doesn't have his wellies on," Mum says.

Dave grins. "Didn't stop him."

Mum rolls her eyes at Dave. "Maybe the responsible adult with him should have. Come here, Alex; let's get you out of those soggy clothes."

"Feel like fleeing the bedlam?" Clover whispers to me.

I nod eagerly.

"Sylvie, OK if I take Amy out for pizza?" Clover says easily. "She's had a very stressful day."

"Fine," Mum says as she wrestles Alex out of his damp shirt. A clump of autumn leaves falls to the floor. Mum looks at Dave. "Would you like to explain that?"

He shrugs. "It was a game."

"I don't want to hear any more. Don't be late, Amy," she calls over her shoulder as we escape.

Clover starts the engine, revs it a few times, and then looks over at me. "So where does he live?"

"Who?"

"Mac Otis. I presume that's where this Bailey journey is taking you next. You're not a girl to give up that easily, are you, Bean Machine?"

"But what about Bailey? He said to leave him alone."

Clover sighs. "What boys say and what boys mean are two different things, my friend. Have I taught you nothing? And it really can't make things any worse, not now."

"Where have I heard that before?" I murmur.

"Look, Bailey lives with this Mac guy, right? At the very least you should tell him what happened today — give him a heads-up in case Bailey does anything stupid."

"You're right. But I'm scared, Clover. He's probably Gramps's age. What will I say?"

"Tell him the truth, Beanie, plain and simple. Always best." She pauses and then corrects herself: "Mostly anyway. A few white lies never hurt anyone."

"Like telling Mum you were taking me for pizza?"

"*Exactement*. And I am, Beanie, later. See, only a white lie." She grins and presses down on the accelerator.

I'm standing outside Valhalla, Marine Terrace, Bray — Mac and Bailey's place — quaking in my Converse. I glance back at Clover, who is parked across the street. I left her text-flirting with Brains. She offered to come with me, but this is something that I need to do alone.

Feeling my gaze, she lifts her head, buzzes down the window, and gives me a reassuring smile and wave.

After taking a deep breath, I press the bell. It rings in the bowels of the old Georgian house. After a few seconds, I hear the sound of someone walking toward the door. It swings open. I'm relieved to see it's not Bailey standing there. The man is about sixty with a lived-in face, closely cropped white hair, and a strong jaw. He's wearing a crumpled blue shirt and jeans. "Yes?" he asks. His gray-blue eyes look tired.

"Is this where Bailey Otis lives?" I ask nervously.

"Yes." He sighs. "What kind of trouble is he in this time?"

"Oh no, nothing like that. He's in my class at Saint John's. We're friends."

"Friends? Really?" He tilts his head. He seems surprised.

"Are you Mac?"

"Aye, that's right."

"Look, there's something I need to tell you. About Bailey."

He looks at me for a moment. "You don't know where he is, by any chance? Haven't had sight nor sound of him since lunchtime."

It's like someone's stabbed me in the gut. What have I done? "No, but I did see him earlier. On Killiney Beach."

Just say it, Amy, I tell myself. *If Bailey's run off or something's happened to him, it'll be all your fault.*

"He bumped into Finn Hunter—"

Mac cuts me off. "Did you say Finn Hunter?" His eyes bore into mine.

I nod wordlessly.

"You'd best come in." He stands back, and I walk into the narrow hall.

My hands are shaking with nerves. I know it's only a matter of time until I'll have to come clean about my involvement.

Inside, there's a console table littered with junk

mail and an overflowing laundry basket sitting in the middle of the floor. Mac kicks the basket aside and leads me to the kitchen at the back of the house. Light floods in through plate-glass windows. Outside, a trampoline dwarfs the scruffy garden, and I smile to myself. I can't imagine Bailey on a trampoline — but it doesn't look all that old.

Mac sees me looking at it. "Bailey's out there bouncing every evening — even in the rain — listening to his music. Double flips, somersaults, the works; he's completely fearless. Sometimes the neighbors' kids hear the springs and climb over the wall to join in. Bailey doesn't mind; he seems to like the company. He's great with kids. Says they don't ask stupid questions." He stops and rubs his face with his hands. "I guess you'd better start at the beginning. Take a seat."

He pulls out a kitchen chair, and I sit down. There's a mess of newspapers and music magazines on the table.

"Would you like a drink?" he asks. "A Coke or something?"

I shake my head.

"Mind if I make myself a coffee before we talk?"

My stomach lurches when he says the word *talk*.

Why am I putting myself through this? It was such a bad idea. I want to get up and run. *Stop being such a chicken, Amy,* I tell myself.

As Mac makes coffee in a cafetière, I look around. The kitchen's long and narrow, with a large stainless-steel range to the right, framed by open metal shelving that is filled with professional-looking copper pots and pans.

I sweep my eyes toward the white shelving unit to the left. It is crammed with dozens of cookbooks. Then something else catches my eye: a small silver statue of a man on a plinth. A bit like an Oscar, except the figure is playing a guitar. I peer at the plaque on the base: "Young Songwriter of the Year."

"Bailey won that," Mac says in a quiet voice. "Beat a whole load of sixteen- and seventeen-year-olds, too. That was before all the Lakelands trouble, of course . . . How much has he told you, Amy?"

"Practically nothing. Was he expelled?"

"He was, I'm afraid. Some boy was teasing him about his ancient dad — I guess he meant me — and Bailey threw a punch and knocked out one of the lad's front teeth. Bailey tends to lash out when he can't cope with his feelings." Mac gives a dry laugh. "It's how he expresses himself. That and his music.

Anyway, you'd better tell me what happened with Finn. Did Finn contact Bailey directly—ask if he could meet him, that it?"

"Not exactly." I gulp. "It was my fault. My aunt's a journalist, and she requested an interview with Finn. Asked him to meet us on Killiney Beach for a photo shoot—"

"Knowing Bailey would be there teaching his kids," Mac puts in. "I get it. But what I don't understand is how you know about Finn and Bailey. Bailey would hardly have told you."

I consider lying, spinning Mac some story about Clover's "research," but something stops me. I guess I figure there have been enough lies and misunderstandings already.

"My mum's ghostwriting Finn's memoir," I say truthfully. "I read her notes and some of Bailey's letters to Finn."

Mac's eyes harden. "Those are private letters, young lady. You had no right."

"I know—and I'm sorry. I thought if they met face-to-face, things might be different. I thought it was worth a try, but I made a mistake."

"And what happened? Did they speak to each other?"

"Finn tried talking to him, but Bailey was having

none of it. He told Finn to leave him alone" — I take a deep breath — "and then, he, um, punched Finn in the jaw and ran off."

Mac swears under his breath and then gives a deep sigh. "I see. Look, I'm sure you were only trying to help, but that was inevitable, I'm afraid. Bailey's put up a wall around himself, and nothing can smash it down — not me and certainly not Finn Hunter. Jennie, my ex-wife, she fed the lad all these notions: stupid fairy tales about finding his dad and patching everything up. It was all nonsense, and it only made things worse. She made Bailey write dozens of letters to the man. Finn never wrote back, not once. Contacted me months afterward, of course. Said his mum had never forwarded the letters on. I didn't believe a word of it. Finn's just too selfish to care about anyone except himself. Always was, even as a teenager."

"But it is true! Finn knew nothing about the letters until after his mum died. He's moved back to Dublin to try to patch things up with Bailey. And he was genuinely devastated on the beach after Bailey ran off."

"Why didn't you just tell Finn where the lad would be and leave the rest up to him, then? Why did you have to trick him onto the beach like that? Eh?"

"Maybe I should have, but I didn't. I'm so sorry." I stand up, blinking back my tears. "I was wrong to come here. I just wanted you to know that Bailey's upset, that was all. I think he was crying when he ran off."

Mac nods, his face softening. "It took a lot of courage to come here. Bailey . . ." He shakes his head. "He's not easy. He's hurt and he's been through so much. His mum, Lane, was just the same. Difficult. Had these notions about how her life should be but wasn't prepared to put the work in. She wanted to be a singer but felt having Bailey had put the kibosh on that. Finally she just ran out on the poor lad."

He sighs and looks directly at me, his eyes sad. "I should probably warn you off Bailey — tell you to keep your distance, but he's my grandson and he's all the family I've got. Promise me you'll keep an eye on him. He doesn't seem to have many friends. Maybe you'll ring me if anything happens in school next week?"

"Of course."

"And don't worry about him too much. He has a habit of wandering off. I'm sure he'll reappear later. I'll give you a call if he doesn't."

"Thanks."

We exchange numbers, and then Mac shows me out.

I walk back to the car with a heavy heart.

"You OK, Beanie?" Clover asks gently.

"That was one of the hardest things I've ever had to do," I admit.

"Was he angry?"

"At first, but then he was just sad. I'll tell you about it later, OK? Can you just take me home, Clover? I don't fancy eating right now."

"'Course, I understand. I'm proud of you, Beanie. We all make mistakes; it's how you deal with them that matters. Remember that."

♥ *Chapter 18*

School on Monday is horrible; I can't get Bailey's story out of my head. In English class I keep trying to catch his eye, but I think he's purposefully avoiding my gaze. Still, I'm glad he's in school. He didn't run away — at least that's something.

At the end of break, I'm walking toward my locker with Mills and Seth when Mills suddenly grabs my arm. "What's Bailey up to?"

I look up to see Bailey smashing what looks suspiciously like *my* hockey stick against the door of *my* locker. He takes another swing.

"Bailey!" Mills yells. "What are you doing?"

He turns around and their eyes meet.

Mills gulps. I know she still has strong feelings for Bailey, even though she tries to hide it.

"I hate this place," he says. "It's the pits." His eyes bore into mine; his are dark and swirling with anger and despair. "And I hate *you*."

"Look, Bailey—" Seth says.

But Bailey cuts him off. "You don't know what it's like, being trapped here." And he brings the hockey stick down again. *WHACK!* I stare at the shaft. Yep, it's mine, all right: a silver Voodoo stick with "AG" written in black marker just above the head. (I'd left it on top of the lockers this morning, never for a minute thinking it would become a weapon of mass destruction!)

"That's my stick, Bailey," I say. "You're going to ruin it *and* my locker."

Bailey gives a hollow laugh. "That's the general idea." He hits the metal door again.

"Look, I'm so sorry about Saturday," I say quickly. "I'd never do anything to deliberately hurt you. You've got to—" But I'm interrupted mid-sentence.

"Bailey Otis, what on earth are you doing?" Loopy is staring at him, looking distressed. "That locker is school property. There's no excuse for vandalism. I've a good mind to send you to Mr. Montgomery."

Bailey drops his head and gazes at the floor.

"It's my fault, miss," I say quickly.

She looks at me. "Really, Amy? And why's that?"

"I . . . er . . . asked Bailey to try to open the locker for me. I've lost the key."

Loopy looks back at Bailey. "Is that right, Bailey?"

"Yeah," he says to the floor tiles.

"And Mills? What's your role in all this?" Loopy asks.

Mills gives a little gasp. She *never* gets in trouble in school. "Innocent bystander, miss," she says. "Honest. Seth too."

Loopy sighs. "It's a pretty stupid thing to do, Bailey. And, Amy, for heaven's sake, why didn't you just call Mr. Joey? He's quite used to sawing off locks." (Mr. Joey is the school janitor.)

I shrug. "Didn't think of that, miss."

"Clearly. I don't know what to do with the pair of you. I have to give you some sort of punishment, I suppose . . ." She trails off, chewing on her lip. Discipline isn't Loopy's strong point.

"Detention, miss?" I say glumly.

She shakes herself. "Gosh, no, no. Complete waste of everyone's time and energy." She looks carefully at Bailey. His head is still low and his face pale. "I'll let you off this time. I'll send Mr. Joey up to deal with your lock, Amy, and the rather alarming dents in that door. Luckily for you, he's an expert panel beater. But no more shenanigans, Mr. Otis, understand? Are you trying to get yourself expelled?"

"Maybe," he murmurs. He drops the stick on the floor with a clatter, then turns on his heels and walks away.

Loopy's eyes follow him down the corridor. She mutters something under her breath that sounds suspiciously like "That poor boy." To me, she says, "You all right, Amy? Your eyes look rather red."

"She has conjunctivitis, miss," Mills says, covering for me.

Loopy gives a doubtful "hmm," then says, "Right, run along to class now, all of you."

As soon as Loopy has gone, Mills and Seth both look at me. My eyes are still teary. I was only trying to help Bailey, but instead I've made things a hundred times worse. Again.

"What's going on, Amy?" Mills asks gently. "What happened on Saturday? Why did Bailey freak out like that?"

It's time to tell Mills and Seth the truth.

"We need to talk." I usher them behind the lockers, away from prying eyes. We all sit down and lean our backs against the wall.

"It's complicated," I begin. "You know Mum's

been working on Finn Hunter's memoir? I read her notes and, well, to cut a long story short: Bailey is Finn's son. Finn ran off to London when Bailey's mum was pregnant. It gets worse, though. When he was only three, Bailey's mum ran off too." I stop and look from Mills to Seth and then back at Mills. They're staring at me in complete and utter shock. I had been planning to tell them the whole story — about Bailey being Baby X and everything. But now the moment is here, I can't do it. To Mills, to Seth, or to Bailey.

I know hearing about it would devastate Mills; she has such a sheltered view of the world, and I don't want to be the one to shatter her illusions. And with Polly in and out of the hospital, Seth has enough to worry about. Clover and Mum are different — they're strong, like me, and they're not as close to Bailey. Besides, would Bailey really want so many people knowing about his past? It must be painful enough as it is.

No, for the moment, Bailey's past is a secret I'll have to carry without Mills's and Seth's help.

"Poor Bailey. What happened to him then, Amy?" Mills looks completely stricken. I was right not to tell her all the details.

"He had to go and live with his grandpa. Mac.

The guy you thought was his dad, Seth." I tell them about Bailey's unanswered letters to Finn.

"Oh, Amy," Mills whispers. She's so overcome, she can't say anything else. Tears start running down her cheeks, and she wipes them away with her fingers.

"I know." I pat her shoulder.

"Christ," Seth says. "Imagine your own father rejecting you not once but twice. And your mum too."

"There's more . . ." I say, even though there's a lump the size of an orange in my throat — and I tell them everything that happened on Killiney Beach. "It was a disaster," I finish. "I've made such a mess of things."

Seth and Mills exchange a loaded look. Seth gives her a tiny frown and puts his arm around my shoulder.

"You were only trying to help, Amy," he says kindly. "Don't blame yourself. Hey, it might have worked."

"But what now?" Mills says. "Bailey must hurt so much, and there's nothing we can do about it."

"I know," I say. "And that's the worst thing of all. None of us can help him. He's pushed everyone who cares about him away, even Mac. I don't know what's going to happen to him."

"Oh, Amy, it's horrible." Mills swipes at her flooded eyes with the edge of her sleeve. "I'm sorry — it's just so sad."

"Come here," Seth says, putting one arm around me and the other around Mills. "We all need to stick together today."

♥ Chapter 19

The following Sunday the home phone rings. Dave's out walking the babies and Mum's at the supermarket, so I roll off the sofa, walk into the hall, and pick up the handset. "Yello? Green and Wildgust residence. How may I help you?"

"Amy, it's Mac. You haven't seen Bailey today, by any chance, have you? He snuck out early this morning. There's still no sign of him, and he's not answering his mobile. He didn't say one word to me yesterday — he was really moody. I'm starting to get seriously worried."

My stomach clenches like a fist. Mac sounds completely freaked out.

"I haven't seen him since school on Friday, I'm afraid," I say. "He's not really talking to any of us at the moment, least of all me. If he makes contact, though, I'll let you know immediately."

"Thanks, Amy. I hope he hasn't done anything stupid. I've been driving around for hours. I've tried Bray Head, the seafront, the arcades — there's no sign of him anywhere. Can you think of anywhere else I should look?"

"Not really. Do you think it has something to do with what happened on the beach? Seeing Finn?"

There's a long pause. "I don't know, lass. He was acting strange even before that, so don't fret too much."

I put down the phone, the words "I hope he hasn't done anything stupid" ringing in my ears. I chew on my lip. This isn't good — even though Mac said not to blame myself, it's hard not to.

I ring Seth. "Bailey's missing again," I say as soon as he picks up. "Mac just rang. He hasn't seen him since early this morning. I don't suppose he's been in touch with you?"

"Nope."

I sigh. "This is all my fault. What if he's run away? To London or something, like Finn did."

"He wouldn't do something like that, would he? Not without telling anyone . . . OK, maybe he would. What about those kids he teaches at the beach, though? He wouldn't just leave without telling them, surely."

"The *beach*!" I cry. "He's on Killiney Beach. I just know it. It's his safe place: the only place he's happy. It's really windy today too. I bet he's gone surfing. Maybe he's in trouble. What if he got swept out to sea on a wave or something?"

"I'm sure he's fine, Amy. He knows what he's doing. But we'd better go and check anyway. I'll meet you at the Martello Tower in twenty minutes, yeah?"

"See you there. I'll grab Mills on the way."

As soon as I've hung up, I dash out the back door to grab my bike from the shed. One of the tires is completely flat. "*Póg, póg,* and triple *póg,*" I mutter, kicking the saggy wheel. I throw it onto the grass and run over to Mills's house instead. No one is answering the bell, so I slap the door with the flat of my hand. "Come on, come on!"

"Hold your horses!" Mills says as she swings the door open. She stares at me. "Amy, what's wrong?"

"Is your mum in?" I ask her frantically. "Can she give us a lift to Killiney Beach?"

"No, the parentals have gone to buy a cherry tree in some special garden center in Wicklow. What's on at Killiney Beach?"

"Bailey's missing and I think he's on the beach and my bike's busted and we need to get there fast. Any ideas?"

"We could get the train . . ."

I shake my head. "There are *siúcra* all trains on a Sunday. No, there has to be another—"

I stop mid-sentence, and Mills and I simultaneously say, "Clover!"

Clover isn't answering her mobile, so I ring the home phone.

"Hello, Autumn House. How can I help you?" It's Gramps.

"Gramps, it's Amy. Is Clover there?"

"No, she's out with Brains. Howth Head, I think they said. Romantic walk."

Darn. Howth's miles away. "Gramps, I need a favor. Can you pick me up from Mills's house, like right now, and take us to Killiney Beach? It's urgent."

He laughs. "Late for a hot date, Amy Damey, that it?"

"Something like that. Please, Gramps?" I beg.

"Sounds vital. Normally I'd love to help you out, but the car's in the garage until Tuesday."

"AAAUUUGGGHHH!"

"You OK, Amy?"

"Not really, but don't worry—I'll think of something."

I click off my phone and turn to Mills. "Do you have any money?"

"Not much—just some change."

"And I have about ten euro. Let's hope it's enough. We're going to have to get a taxi. Nothing else to do . . ."

We dash back to my house—and bump into Mum, who is walking up the path, her arms laden down with shopping bags. "Where are you pair off to in such a hurry?" she asks.

"Bailey's gone missing, Mum," I explain quickly. "We think he's on Killiney Beach."

Mum studies my face. "How long has he been gone?"

"Since early this morning. Mac's been looking for him for hours. He said Bailey was acting weird all day yesterday too."

"Mac? You've been talking to Bailey's grandpa?"

"Can I fill you in later, Mum? Right now, we need to concentrate on finding Bailey."

"I understand. Hop in," she says, nodding at the car. "I'll drive you." After dumping the shopping bags in the trunk, she jumps into the driver's seat. I climb into the passenger seat, and Mills sits in the back, wedged between the two car seats.

"Won't the ice cream melt?" I ask.

"Some things are more important," Mum says, pressing her foot on the accelerator and reversing down the path at full speed. "Besides, it'll refreeze. Alex and Evie have iron stomachs."

"Now," she says as she pulls onto Glenageary Road. "It's time to come clean about Mac, Amy."

"I went over last weekend," I begin. "To tell him about the whole Finn and Bailey business. And to apologize for getting involved."

"And?"

"He was pretty annoyed at first, but then he softened up. He's not a bit impressed with Finn, though. Called him selfish."

"I can imagine. Running off on his only daughter like that. But Finn *has* changed."

The car in front of us is doing about twenty miles an hour. "Get a move on," Mum mutters, gripping the steering wheel. Then suddenly she rams her foot down and overtakes it.

"Way to go, Mum." I laugh.

Mum's always complaining about Clover's rally-car driving tendencies, but I can see where Clover gets them from now. Speed greed must run in the Wildgust family.

I catch Mills's eye in the rearview mirror. She looks a little shaken by Mum's driving. Luckily we're nearly at the beach now.

"Which end of the beach?" Mum asks as we roar down the hill.

"The Bray end. We're meeting Seth at the Martello Tower."

"Roger that," Mum says, and pulls to a screeching halt on the side of the road. "I'm coming with you."

"We'll be fine, Mum," I protest — but Mills shrugs. "We might need her," she says in a quiet voice.

I guess she's right.

After Mum has locked the car — not that anyone would want to steal it — the three of us run toward the Martello Tower. Mum's surprisingly fast; she's leaving me and Mills in the dust. Must be all the practice she gets tearing after Alex and Evie. However, by the time we reach the tower, she's doubled over with the effort, puffing and panting.

"No . . . sign of . . . Seth yet," I say to Mills, my own breath a little raggedy.

"Now what?" she asks.

"We start looking for Bailey. Seth can catch up with us when he arrives."

"Which way? Should we split up?"

I nod. "I'll take the Bray end with Mum. You walk toward White Rock. Yell if you see anything—or if I'm out of earshot, ring me."

"Got it." And Mills starts walking down the beach, her head sweeping from side to side as she scans the beach and water carefully, looking for Bailey.

Mum and I head the other way. My mind is racing: What if we don't find him? What if I'm wrong about the beach? Bailey could be halfway to France on the ferry by now. I wonder if Mac has checked for his passport.

"He'll turn up, Amy," Mum says gently, as though reading my mind. She strokes my cheek gently, and for once I don't pull away. "You have to stop blaming yourself. For now, let's just concentrate on scouring the beach, OK?"

We walk on in silence, and as Mum suggested, I focus on the beach. I spot a dark-haired boy near the water, and for a brief second my heart lifts. But when I run toward him, I realize he's much smaller than Bailey and wearing a Manchester United T-shirt, which Bailey wouldn't be seen dead in.

Dead.

The word lingers in my head even as I try to shake it away. I look around for Mum, but she has peeled off to the right, searching the sand dunes, so I keep walking along the shoreline. The tide's on its way out, leaving damp curves on the pebbles. Feeling more and more frustrated, I kick a stone into the sea.

"Amy!" someone calls behind me, and I spin around. Seth's running toward me. "I thought you were going to wait for me at the tower," he says.

"Sorry, I wanted to start looking for Bailey. Mills is trying the other end of the beach, and Mum's checking out the dunes. But this is pointless. He could be anywhere. What if he never comes back, Seth? I should never have interfered. I'm so stupid."

Seth pushes my hair back off my face. "Amy, I think your instinct's right. This beach is about the only place he feels happy at the moment, and he loves teaching those kids. But we need to keep looking. We're not doing any good standing here, worrying."

I nod, and we start walking silently up the beach, side by side. Then suddenly Seth stops dead. "Is that a surfboard?" he asks.

A blue-and-white board is lying in the marram grass, a black rucksack beside it. I riffle through the bag and pull out a black T-shirt with a skull design and a wet suit.

"It's Bailey's T-shirt. I've seen him in it." Seth looks concerned. "But where's Bailey?"

179 ♥

And it's then that I spot something in the waves. A boy with jet-black hair is standing shoulder deep in the water, staring out to sea.

It's Bailey!

"But what's he doing?" Seth asks when I point out Bailey to him. "He's not moving." Seth pauses for a second, then says, "I'm going in," and ripping off his T-shirt, jeans, and Converse, he runs down the beach.

I run after him. He winces as his bare feet hit the pebbles, but he doesn't let it slow him down, and he enters the water quickly. "Shoot, it's freezing," he says as he begins to wade toward Bailey while I wait on the beach. "Hey, Bailey, what are you doing?" I hear him call. "You'll turn into an ice cube if you stay in any longer, man."

Bailey doesn't turn around, so Seth continues out to sea until he's next to him. Seth keeps talking, but Bailey still isn't shifting. Finally, Seth looks back at me and puts his hands in the air as if to say, *What now?*

"You have to get out of the water, Bailey!" I shout. "You'll get hypothermia. Seth, tell him."

Seth says something in a low, soothing voice, snatches of which drift back toward me on the wind. "Talk to me, mate . . . Say something . . . Your teeth . . . chattering . . . Your . . . blue . . . Come on . . . don't be stupid."

Seth looks back at me again, his face panicked. "He won't budge!" he yells.

"Then you'll have to pull him out."

"OK, I'll try." Seth puts his arms around Bailey's upper body. At his touch, Bailey suddenly comes to life, thrashing about and elbowing Seth in the face.

"Ow!" Seth shouts. "What are you doing? That hurt."

"I'm coming in," I yell, throwing my jacket down on the pebbles. As it lands with a thud, I remember that my iPhone is in my pocket. *Siúcra!* I hope I haven't smashed the screen. Plus, I've forgotten to ring Mills and to shout at Mum; she'll be halfway to Bray at this stage. Too late now.

I run into the water and gasp as icy fingers seem to prick my feet, then my thighs, my waist, and finally my chest. Seth was right. The water's arctic and deep. I'm on my tiptoes by the time I get to the boys, the waves splashing over my face.

"I can't get him to move," Seth says, his face pale. "Can you still stand?"

"Only just."

"I'll hold you up." He puts his arms around my waist and lifts me up out of the water.

"Bailey, listen to me," I say. Close up, his face is gray and his lips are blue and quivering, and his eyes, which are staring out to sea, are glassy and unfocused. "I'm so sorry about the whole Finn business. It's all my fault."

Finally he opens his mouth and speaks. "No, I'm the one who me-messed it u-up," he says, his words shaky and distorted. "Hitting him like th-th-that. He must h-h-hate me."

"He doesn't hate you, Bailey, I swear," I say. "Please come out of the water before you freeze to death."

"Amy's right," Seth adds. "Come on, buddy."

Bailey just ignores us.

There's a noise from the beach. Turning, I see Mum standing by the edge of the water. "Amy!" she yells. "Is he all right?"

"No! We can't get him out of the water."

"Hang in there." Mum begins wading through the water toward us, still fully clothed.

"He won't move, Mum," I tell her when she's close enough to not have to shout. "We've tried talking to him. It's like he's stuck. He's worried about hitting Finn. Said Finn must hate him."

Mum nods at me. "It's going to be all right, Bailey," she tells him, stroking his head. "I'm Sylvie, Amy's mum. Guess you're having a rough day, yeah?"

Tears burst from his eyes. He lifts a hand to brush them away — but his water-crinkled fingers are shaking so much, he can't move them properly, so Mum does it for him.

"Amy told me what happened on the beach," she says as she does so. "And Finn told me all about it too. It really upset him, but he doesn't blame you for thumping him. And his lip is fine."

I stare at Mum. She didn't say a word about *that*. Finn obviously swore her to secrecy. Bailey's eyes are glued to her too.

"I think Finn needed someone to talk to," Mum continues. "I've been writing your dad's memoir, you see. So I know all about you, Bailey. Finn was devastated that you wouldn't talk to him last weekend. He's determined not to give up, though. He says he has finally figured out that his life isn't worth living unless you're in it."

"But I've r-r-ruined everything," Bailey says. "How can he want me near him n-n-now?"

"Do you know what else he told me?" Mum goes on. "He said there was *nothing* you could do that would make him give up on you. He's changed, Bailey. He's not the scared boy who abandoned you. He's a different person. And he wants to get to know you. So come out of the water, please?"

"But he's f-f-famous. And I'm d-d-damaged goods. S-s-someone will find out about my past, and he'll be t-t-toast. His image will be r-r-ruined."

"I don't think he cares anymore," Mum says earnestly. "He was even talking about putting your letters in the book — with your permission, of course. Or not publishing the book at all if that's what you'd prefer. He just wants you in his life, Bailey, simple as that. And nothing that happened in the past was your fault. Do you understand me? It wasn't your fault. Finn just doesn't want it all dragged up again in case it hurts you. That's all."

"But sh-sh-she left me," Bailey says through chattering teeth. "I must h-h-have done s-s-s-something wrong. I must have been a really d-d-difficult baby."

"No!" Mum says firmly. "You were three, Bailey! You did nothing wrong. It wasn't your fault. I want you to say it — say, 'It wasn't my fault.' Go on, say it. 'It wasn't my fault.'"

Bailey looks at her, stricken.

"Mum's right. It wasn't your fault, Bailey," I say softly. "You were tiny."

"Go on, Bailey," Mum says. "'It wasn't my fault.'"

Tears stream down Bailey's face. "It w-wasn't my f-f-fault," he mouths. Then he says it louder: "It w-wasn't my f-f-fault. It wasn't my f-fault. IT WASN'T MY F-FAULT!" His words rattle out like machine-gun fire, getting louder and louder.

"That's right, Bailey." Mum smiles through her own tears. "Let it all out." Then she hugs him before going on in a low, firm voice: "Now you listen to me, Bailey Otis, and you listen to me good: everyone has their own cross to bear. I lost my mum a few years back, and I thought I'd fall apart. Then my marriage ended, and I did go to pieces. But I got through it, and now things are good. Life isn't easy for anyone, but you have to stick in there, ride the bad times out, and wait for the good ones to come. Because there will be good times. You're only a teenager. You have your whole life ahead of you. So get out of the water, young man. Right now! Or we're all going to die of hypothermia — because we're not leaving you, Bailey."

He shakes his head, his lips mashed together, tears still rolling down his cheeks. "I c-c-c-an't," he says. "I think I'm f-f-f-frozen solid."

"I'll help," Seth says. "Let me carry you."

Bailey closes his eyes and then slowly opens them again. "OK," he whispers.

"Thank God," Mum says. "Now everyone out, quickly."

Seth sweeps Bailey into his arms and, helped by the buoyancy of the water, carries him to the shore. Mum holds my hand, and we pull each other through the waves.

On the beach Seth puts Bailey down gently. Bailey immediately huddles in a ball, shivering violently. It's not surprising—he's wearing a pair of board shorts and nothing else, and from the waxiness of his skin, it's obvious he's been in the water for far too long.

"Should I ring an ambulance?" I ask Mum.

"Yes," she says. "Tell them it's urgent. We need to warm him up now, though, or he may have a heart attack from the cold."

I dial with wet, shaking fingers.

"Emergency services," a calm female voice says. "How can I help?"

"We need an ambulance. It's urgent. It's my friend. We found him in the sea, and he has severe hypothermia. His whole body's rigid, and his lips are blue."

"Breathing?"

"Yes."

"I'll send out an ambulance immediately. Where are you?"

After I give her the details, she says, "Caller, I'm ringing it through now. Please hold the line."

Seconds later she's back. "They're on their way. In the meantime, you must try to keep him warm. But nothing sudden, understand? Keep your phone on and call us if there's any change. We'll be there in about ten minutes."

I click off the call. "They're on their way. The woman said to keep him warm."

Mum has already put my jacket over Bailey's chest and is rubbing his face gently with her hands.

At that moment, Mills appears. "What's happening?" she asks, crouching down beside Bailey. "Why is he that horrible color? Bailey, are you all right? Can you hear me? Oh, what's wrong with him?" She puts her hand over her mouth, and tears spring to her eyes.

Mum says, "Mills, listen to me. It's important. You are the only warm person here. And we need your dry clothes."

"But Bailey—" Mills says, her face crumpling.

"Concentrate, Mills," Mum says. "You're going to lie down and press your skin against Bailey's back. We'll layer all the dry clothes over the pair of you. The rest of us are wet and cold from the water—your body heat might just keep him alive. Seth, you're going to sandwich him. I need you to run around and get as warm as you can."

Seth starts doing jumping jacks and squats to warm up.

Mills's face is a picture. "Do you mean *all* my clothes?"

"Mills, just get on with it," I say. "Leave your bra and knickers on. No one's looking."

"I a-a-am." Bailey manages to give a tiny smile — even though his breathing is ragged and his face is so pale, it's practically translucent.

Reluctantly, Mills strips down. Then under Mum's direction, Seth moves Bailey onto his side.

"Mills, quickly now," Mum says. "Lie down against Bailey's back and push your body hard against his skin."

Mills nods and lies down on the pebbles, wiggling her body forward until as much of her as possible is pressing against his back.

"Holy moly, he's an iceberg," she says.

"That's why he needs your warmth," Mum says patiently.

Seth rolls his eyes at me. I know he finds Mills a bit ditzy sometimes.

"Hang in there, Bailey," Mills whispers. She wraps her arms around him.

Mum turns to Seth. "You warm now?" she asks him.

He nods.

"Good. Press your back right up against Bailey's chest. And then we just have to wait for the paramedics."

As Mum and I cover the three of them with all the dry clothes, a woman in a silk headscarf stops beside us. "Everything all right here?" she asks, her eyes sweeping over the huddle of bodies.

"The lad in the middle has hypothermia," Mum explains. "Spent too long in the water. Ambulance is on its way."

The woman takes off her green puffer jacket and hands it to Mum. "Here, put this over them. Howard!" she shouts at a man holding a chocolate Labrador by its lead near by. "We need your jacket."

He hands it over, and Mum layers the jackets on top of Mills, Bailey, and Seth. The couple sits down on the pebbles and waits for the ambulance with us.

"Do you know the boy?" the woman asks Mum.

"Yes—he's my daughter's friend. He was surfing without a wet suit."

The woman nods. She seems happy with this explanation. But if it was as simple as that, then why didn't Bailey leave the water as soon as he started to get cold? I exchange a look with Mum, and she gives me a gentle smile. "It's going to be all right, Amy," she says softly, seeming to read my mind for the second time today. "Bailey's going to get the help he needs." She doesn't have to say any more. I can tell by her expression that she understands my concern.

After a few minutes, Mum asks Mills, "Does he feel any warmer?"

Mills nods. "I think so, but he's very still. Is he asleep?"

Mum peers down at Bailey and says, "Bailey? Bailey?"

Nothing.

"Bailey?" She shakes his shoulder. "Bailey?"

Still nothing.

Swearing under her breath, she presses his cheek with her hand; her fingertips leave white imprints in his gray skin. "Bailey, can you hear me?" she says loudly. "You have to stay awake."

"Come on, buddy," Seth says. "Wake up."

Bailey gives a low moan. His eyelids flicker but don't open.

There's a shout from farther up the beach, and, looking up, I see that two men and a woman are running toward us. The two men are carrying a stretcher between them.

"How's he doing?" one of the men asks Mum as the other two paramedics crouch down beside Bailey to examine him: one checks his pulse, the other his body temperature. Seth and Mills are still sandwiching him. Mills's cheeks have turned bright red, and I can tell she's not looking forward to standing up half-naked in front of all these strangers.

"Not so good," Mum says. "He's just about conscious. We tried to warm him up as best we could."

"You've all done a great job," the woman says. "His core temperature is slowly rising. He's not out of the danger zone yet, though. We'll need to zip him into a survival bag and get him straight to the hospital."

"It was mainly thanks to my mum," I say proudly. "We just did what she said."

"Well done," the woman tells Mum. "Your quick thinking may just have saved this lad's life."

Mum blushes a little at the compliment. "I saw it on *Casualty*," she admits with a shy smile.

♥ Chapter 20

Mum is fantastic on Monday too. Mills's mum, Sue, is adamant that Mills won't be visiting Bailey in the hospital. She says that school is far too important to miss — but Mum somehow manages to talk her round. "Bailey really needs his friends at the moment," I hear her telling Sue on the phone. "Yes, I know they could get the bus to Tallaght *after* school, but that would take hours, and I'm happy to drive them over today. I'll drop them straight back to class afterward, I promise."

And it works! Sue says Mills can go — but only for half an hour.

Dave's been really sweet all morning too. It was as we were stacking the dishwasher together that

I finally asked him what's been on my mind since yesterday.

"Can people die from hypothermia? Dave, do you think Bailey did it on purpose?"

He nodded. "Unfortunately, yes. But people don't usually try to end things by standing in the sea on a busy beach, Amy. It sounds more like a cry for help. I'm sure Bailey was hoping someone would find him, and knowing as he does now that he has friends he can rely on and who care about him will make a lot of difference."

After breakfast, we pick up Seth (unlike Sue, Polly didn't take any convincing), and Mum drives us all to Tallaght Hospital, where we find Bailey in one of the children's wards: a bright, sunny room with cartoon characters painted on its yellow walls.

He's sitting up in bed, listening to music through his headphones. He's wearing a plain white T-shirt that makes his emerald eyes ping. (I bet he refused to wear pajamas or a hospital gown.) I realize I've only ever seen him in black before or in the Saint John's uniform. He's still vampire pale, but he looks a lot better than he did yesterday.

He takes off his headphones and drops them onto the bed beside him as we come in. "Hey," he says, looking a bit embarrassed.

But if he's embarrassed, then Mills is mortified: her cheeks are ruby red, and she can't stop staring at her feet.

"This is my mum, Sylvie," I say to Bailey. "She drove us over. You met yesterday."

Bailey gives her a nod, his face reddening. "Mac's in the café. He said he'd love to talk to you — to thank you — if . . ." He drops his eyes to the blue cotton blanket on the bed.

"I'll go and join him," Mum says, smiling gently at Bailey. "Leave you lot to catch up. I'll be back in about twenty minutes, Amy, OK? Take care, Bailey," she adds, putting her hand on his shoulder. "I hope I'll see you again soon. You're welcome at our place anytime."

She walks out of the ward, and I stare after her, wondering if the fairies have whisked away my real mum and left this totally cool, understanding woman in her place. She's been amazing over the last two days.

There's silence. In an attempt to remove the awkwardness, I ask brightly: "How are you feeling, Bailey? Still shivering?"

Bailey shrugs. "Only on the inside."

I have no idea what to say to that, but I'm grateful

that his anger toward me seems to have dissolved in the seawater.

After a moment or two, he lifts his head and gives me a half-smile. "Sorry, Amy. I didn't mean to make you feel uncomfortable." And pushing himself up a little in the bed, he goes on: "Thanks for coming. All of you."

He looks at Mills, who bites her lip nervously and then says, "We wanted to be here for you. We're your friends."

"I haven't been much of a friend to any of you recently," Bailey says. "And, Mills, for the record: I never really liked Annabelle—not the way I liked you. And it's all over. I texted her this morning. I'm sorry for hurting you. Hey, I wrote you a song last night. To apologize, you know."

Mills gives a little gasp. "Really?"

He nods. "I'll sing it to you when I get out of here."

I look from Bailey to Mills and back again. Mills is smiling delightedly. Is it really that simple for her? One song and everything's hunky-dory? Seriously? Bailey behaved terribly.

Seth puts his hand on my arm. "Leave it," he whispers. "It's not the time."

I nod at him. It's enough that Seth understands. He knows how protective I am of Mills. Someone has to be. She's such a big softie.

There's silence again. So, me being me, I have to break it. "We're all so sorry about everything that happened to you in the past, Bailey," I say. "And about that stuff on the beach with Finn. You must have been hurting pretty bad to stand in freezing-cold water like that. I mean, you could have —"

"Amy!" Mills hisses. And even Seth is frowning at me.

"Sorry," I murmur. "I shouldn't have said anything."

"No, it's OK," Bailey says. "I'm sick of hiding things. I don't know why I walked into the sea like that. It was weird; I wasn't thinking straight. My mind was racing, and I guess I wanted to feel nothing: for my body and my mind to go numb. I wanted to stop thinking. But the colder my body got, the more my mind raced."

"But you wanted someone to find you, right?" Mills asks quietly.

He stares down at the blue blanket over his legs. "Honestly?" And for a second, the whole ward seems deathly quiet. "Yes," he says finally. "As soon as I heard Seth's and Amy's voices, I kind of snapped out of my trance. And then Amy's mum—" He breaks off and swallows. "What she said really got to me. I mean you guys all cared enough to freeze your butts off in the Irish Sea, so I must be worth something." He shrugs.

"Oh, Bailey, of course you're worth something," Mills says, her eyes filling with tears.

No one says anything else for a while until eventually Bailey says, "Do you ever wish you'd never been born?"

Mills looks shocked. "That's a terrible thing to say."

"No, it's not. I feel like that sometimes," I say gently. "It's normal to feel a bit down every once in a while. When my mum and dad were fighting all the time, I felt pretty awful. And Seth's been through a lot with Polly being sick and everything."

I pause to check that Seth's all right with what I've just said. He gives me a gentle smile, so I continue: "Bailey, here's how I see it. You can carry on hiding from your past, running away from it, or you can look it in the face and say, 'Yep, that happened to me, but I'm not going to let it ruin the rest of my life.'"

Bailey shakes his head. "You don't know what I went through. You don't know who I am."

"Actually, *I* do," I say gently. Our eyes lock; his are full of pain and anguish and worry and regret and fear — it frightens me. But I think he understands that I know everything — about Baby X and his mother — and that I'll never tell Mills or Seth. Bailey will always carry a deep sadness in his heart — an everlasting scar — but hopefully he can learn to live with it. His eyes soften a little, and he gives me a tiny nod.

"Nothing's changed, mate," Seth says cheerfully, breaking the intense atmosphere. "You're still the same old annoying Bailey Otis to us."

We talk for a while longer until Bailey looks at the clock. "I have to go to this counselor woman at ten. They won't let me out otherwise. It's kind of lame . . ." He trails off.

"I went to one once," Seth says, picking at the skin around his thumb. I look at him in surprise. "When Polly first got sick, I wasn't doing so well," he goes on. "The doctor found me someone to talk to. She was nice. It kinda helped. Talking to someone who wasn't involved and didn't know me from Adam." He shrugs. "It can't do any harm, and it might get you off some school, mate."

"Guess so," Bailey says.

I take a deep breath. *Don't do it, Amy,* a little voice is telling me. But if I don't say it now, I never will. And it's important. "Bailey, you should talk to her about Finn. See what she thinks about you two meeting up."

"Yeah, all right." Bailey looks at me. He doesn't seem angry, though, just a little tired.

"So you'll think about it?" (I know, I know; I'm like a dog with a bone.)

Bailey shrugs. "Yes, Greenster. I'll think about it, OK? Just for you." His voice is flat, but his eyes have brightened. There's hope.

♥ Chapter 21

That evening Clover is practically glued to the sofa as I unfold the drama of the last two days.

"*Siúcra ducra*, Beans," she says with a low whistle when I've finished telling her everything. "That's quite the story. Poor old Bailey. I hope he feels stronger soon." She breaks off and picks at a hangnail. "And if that wounded soldier can face his woolly mammoth-size demons, I don't really have any excuse, do I, Bean Machine?"

"Cliona, you mean?"

She nods. "*Exactement*. And the bold Lucas Kendall. *Especially* Kendall. I have to face them both before I can move on. *Visage* to *visage*."

"If it can wait till Wednesday afternoon, I'll go to Trinity with you. Give you a bit of moral support."

"Would you mind? Just thinking about it gives me the collywobbles, but I'm sick of hiding between lectures and missing out on all the college parties. Paddy keeps asking me to write for the mag using a pseudonym, and I hate turning him down. But either I write as Clover Wildgust, or I don't write at all. I'm not hiding my identity for anyone. Plus the Trinity Ball's on soon. Don't want to be Cinderella, leaving when my spell wears off at midnight, now, do I?"

"Spell?"

She sighs. "Confidence spell. Every morning I stand in front of the mirror and tell myself that Cliona and Kendall won't bother me — that today will be the day I'll shimmer past them, cool as a Bacardi Breezer."

"Does it work?"

"Never. But as I always say, life moves pretty fast: if I'm not careful, my college years will have whizzed right by me. No, it's finally time to face my fears."

Bailey still isn't back in school by Wednesday. I haven't heard from him, but he's been in contact with Seth. Apparently, Bailey's new counselor has suggested he take some time off to get his strength back. Physical strength or mental strength, I didn't like to ask.

Mills is on cloud nine. Bailey has been texting her every day. She knows I don't approve, but she says she has to tell someone or she'll burst. I just hope he doesn't trample on her heart again.

After school I take the DART to Pearse Street and nip into the loo to change out of my uniform and into skinny jeans, Converse, and the soft gray leather jacket Clover bequeathed to me on Monday night (which was why she'd called over in the first place). "Extended loan," she'd told me. "I'm bored of it. I'm hoping seeing it on you will give me clothes envy and I'll want it back again."

There is this weird ice-blue light in the loos that makes everything glow like Casper the Friendly Ghost, and I can't get out of there fast enough, so I have to stop outside the college and make Clover hold my tiny makeup mirror while I dab on some lip gloss and mascara. (I met her just outside the train station, and she's jitterbug nervous.)

"Don't know why you're bothering with the gloop, Beanie," she says. "Hate to say it, but you're far too young for most college guys."

"I'm not interested in college guys; it's *my* confidence spell," I say. "Humor me."

"In that case, hold still"—she whips out her cute Benefit makeup case—"and shut your eyes." Sticking one of the mini eyeshadow brushes in her mouth, she prepares to get to work with the other. I close my eyes, and she starts tickling my lids with the brushes.

"What do you think?" she asks when she's done. I examine her work in the mirror.

"Smokin'," I say with a grin.

She smiles. "Smoky eyes I can do. Taught by the master herself — Saffron Cleaver."

"Saffron Cleaver?"

"Saffy. You know, my editor. Scary but awesome. She's part of the reason I've had enough gumption to be here today. I asked her about *Trinity Tatler*, and she had some brilliant ideas about how to revitalize the magazine. She told me to get myself in gear and to start sending them feature ideas, pronto, or she'd whip my behind." (*Good for Saffy*, I think.) "And speaking of awesome, there's Paddy. Hey, Paddser!"

He waves and starts walking toward us. Today he's wearing tartan shorts teamed with a sunny yellow T-shirt and emerald-green high-tops. The guy must live in shorts — whatever the weather.

"How did the basketball game go?" Clover asks him. "Did you win?"

"Sure did. Annihilated UCD." He pretends to dribble a ball with his hand and score a basket.

Basketball! No wonder he has such strong-looking legs.

"You remember Paddy, Amy?"

"How could I forget?" I smile.

He smiles back, his dark eyes shining. "And I certainly haven't forgotten you, my sweet petunia." He takes my hand and kisses it while I giggle. "Now, Clover," he continues, "please tell me you've changed your mind about the magazine and are down at this end of Trinity seeking me out."

"Let's just say I'm considering your offer," Clover says. "But I don't do pen names — it's Clover Wildgust or nothing — so I have to talk to Cliona first."

"Angels in the heavens be praised." Paddy grins. "I don't know what's changed your mind, tooty fruit, but frankly I don't care. I have so many ideas, and it'll be great to have someone on the team to share them with. I'm itching to get started."

"Chickens and hatching and eggs, and all that," Clover says. "I'd better get this over with. Is Cliona in the office?"

"Unfortunately, yes. I'll escort you ladies. But I've got to warn you: Miss Bang isn't in the best of moods. This way."

Clover hangs back and grabs my arm. Panic is dancing all over her face. "Amy, I don't think I can go through with this," she whispers. "I think I'm going to throw up."

"You most certainly can," I say. "Remember Bailey, Clover."

"Yes." She takes a deep breath. "OK. If I don't do this now, I never will."

We follow Paddy toward the *Tatler*'s glass-fronted office nestled under the railway arches. At the door, Paddy looks back at Clover. "Coming in, sweet cakes?"

"I need a second to steel my nerves," she tells him. "You go ahead."

He walks in, leaving the door ajar for her. I wait while she twists her butterfly ring round and round her finger and takes several deep breaths: collecting herself. She's still standing on the threshold when a voice from inside yells, "For heaven's sake, Paddy, it's not our fault she tripped at the Model of the Future competition, is it?"

It's Cliona in full swing.

"Fine, but I'm not writing about the poor girl's crying jag onstage," Paddy says. "And do we have to do a whole two pages on the event? Can't we cover some of the gigs instead? Several people submitted reviews, and some of them are pretty good."

Cliona sighs. "No, we can't. The modeling competition is important. And the fall is what makes the story interesting: gives it edge. Models are always falling off their heels. It comes with the territory. Look at Naomi Campbell and Agyness Deyn—they both picked themselves up and carried on as if nothing had happened. True professionals. Ramona Yong sat on the stage and cried like a baby, and yet she *still* won the blasted modeling contract! There's no justice in this world."

"She was the best girl by miles," Paddy says. "And she had to stop; she'd broken her ankle!"

"And? The show must go on. I typed up a whole edition with a broken finger last year."

Paddy laughs wryly. "Cliona, you bruised it trying to pinch Brian O'Driscoll's buttocks in a nightclub. Hardly the same thing. Look, I'm really not comfortable—"

"I'll give the piece to somebody else if it bothers you." Cliona snatches a piece of paper off Paddy's desk and hands it to the D4 from registration day, Amber Horsefell.

"Write my notes up as a news piece, please, Amber," Cliona says. "And make sure you include the bit about Ramona crying."

Amber blinks a few times and looks at Paddy nervously from under her eyelashes. Cliona was always bossy, but being editor seems to have really gone to her head. I don't remember her being *so* stroppy.

"Now, please!" Cliona says. "We have a deadline, guys. Everything has to be ready by five today, or we'll miss our printing slot."

"It's OK," Paddy tells Amber kindly. "I'll finish typing up the editorial for you."

"Leave it. I'll do it myself in a few minutes." Cliona rolls her eyes and looks around the room. Finally she notices Clover lingering in the doorway.

"In or out?" she asks. "Don't just hover there like an eejit, Clover. I've changed my mind. I could do with a writer who isn't afraid to tell the truth." She looks pointedly at Paddy.

"I'd like to write for the magazine," Clover says, her voice quivering with nerves. "But I need to talk to you first. In private."

Cliona glares at her and then gives a nervy laugh. "OK, but let's make it quick. Deadlines — you know how it is." As she walks outside to join Clover, I move quickly toward a bike a few yards away. Crouching over, I pretend to fiddle with the gearbox. Luckily, Cliona hasn't spotted me yet — I don't want her to tease Clover about bringing me with her. Right at this second, Clover needs all the gumption she can muster.

"Well?" Cliona folds her arms across her chest.

Clover sucks in her breath loudly and then says in a whoosh, "I want to work on the magazine — but on my terms. I want to generate ideas, write features: be properly involved."

Cliona shakes her head. "Not going to happen, Clover, sorry. You can type up the listings and some of my pieces, but that's all that's on offer at the moment."

"But why? You know I can write. And I have some brilliant suggestions for making the magazine even better. Ideas to help boost the readership numbers and bring in more advertising."

Cliona snorts. "Modest too."

"Modest smodest. You *know* I'm good, Cliona."

Cliona smiles, and for a second I see a glimmer of their old friendship. They always loved verbal sparring.

Clover sighs. "I was hoping it wouldn't come to this. But let's face it, you owe me."

"Owe you? Why exactly?"

"Hello? You know exactly why. Besides, you have to give me a chance. Paddy checked the magazine's submission policy. You have to consider articles and reviews sent in by *any* Trinity student; it's in the rules."

Cliona puts her hands on her hips. "I've just offered you a perfectly acceptable role on the mag, it's not my problem if you don't want to take it. The *Trinity Tatler* is fine just the way it is — we don't need new ideas or any new writers."

"That's exactly what we need," Paddy says, appearing in the doorway. "Cliona, I hate to point it out, but under your guidance, the magazine is on its knees. Our grant will be pulled unless we find more readers, and fast. We have to make changes. For a start, I'd like a chance to make some proper editorial decisions. You've been running the magazine like a dictatorship, and it's not right."

Then surprisingly, Amber joins in. "I'm with Paddy on this one. I think we need a good shake-up. I say we make Paddy your coeditor. And," she adds sheepishly, "I have some ideas too."

"And me," another girl says, coming outside to stand beside Amber.

Within seconds, the whole *Tatler* office is outside. Clover moves to stand among the staff. She faces Cliona. "Are you going to join us?" she asks. "Please? Together we can make the *Trinity Tatler* the best college magazine in Ireland."

Cliona shakes her head. "It won't work. I know what you're like, Clover. You'll only try to take over. Make everyone do things your way."

"You're wrong, Cliona," Clover says firmly. "Magazines work best when everyone works together as a team. I've learned that from experience."

"I'm not working with you. My mind's made up." Cliona looks at Paddy. "But yes, you can be coeditor, OK, Paddy? I could do with some help."

"I'll only do it if Clover's on the editorial team too," Paddy says firmly. "In fact, if you don't instate her immediately, I'll resign."

Cliona's face falls — I don't think she was expecting that. "You can't resign. I need you. Look, this is ridiculous. If you're all so worried about the magazine, why didn't you say something to me before? You can't just land it on me now."

"Believe me, we've tried, Cliona," Paddy says. "You're not the easiest person to talk to. Look, why don't we set up a proper editorial panel? Share the responsibility. You can still be overall editor if it makes you happy, so long as the rest of us get to make some of the decisions too — and I want Clover on board as features editor. I'm not budging on that."

"But what about Amber?" Cliona says. "She's the features editor."

"I'm happy to do the listings," Amber says, "if I can also submit some fashion pieces. I'm way out of my depth at the moment, and it would be a relief to hand it over, to be honest."

Clover smiles at Amber. "If you're sure? It sounds like a plan. What do you think, Cliona?"

Cliona knows she's beaten. "We can give it a go, but I'll blame you and Paddy, Clover, if it doesn't work." She claps her hands. "Now back to work, everyone. Chop, chop. We have a magazine to put to bed."

Everyone except Cliona and Clover starts to move back inside. Paddy puts his hand on Clover's arm. "Welcome aboard, doll face. See you inside. I'll clear you a desk."

Once he's gone, Cliona leans in toward Clover. "For the record, I'm sorry about . . . everything. Kendall was never right for you—in your heart you know that."

"You hurt me, Cliona," Clover says simply. "We were supposed to be best friends."

Cliona's eyes are softer now. "I know, but all's fair in love and war, eh? For the record, I miss you. All the time."

I watch them, wondering if they'll hug and make up, but then someone calls, "Cloves? Cloves?"

211 ♥

Lucas Kendall is walking toward them, looking as god-like as ever. I study Clover's face, expecting the worst, but she looks calm and collected. She's just standing there, looking at him a little curiously, as if he was just someone she used to know a long time ago, not the boy who crushed her heart.

"Hey, Cloves," he says awkwardly, and gives a long whistle. "It's been a . . . long time."

"Hi, Kendall," she replies. "And, yes, it has."

"So . . . everything OK now? I mean, you and Cliona have finally buried the hatchet, yeah?"

"Everything's fine, Kendall," Clover says coldly. "As you say, it's been a long time."

"And Clover's joining the *Tatler*," Cliona tells him. "She's going to be the new features editor."

"Cool," Kendall says, avoiding eye contact.

Cliona digs him in the ribs. "I'll meet you in the Arts Building in an hour," she says firmly. "I have a few more things to do here first. And I want to talk to Clover. Alone."

He seems keen to get away. Clover's eyes follow him as he heads across campus, but then she turns back to Cliona and sticks out her hand. "Colleagues, then," she says.

Cliona shakes it. "I guess so. And for what it's worth, I really am sorry. Is there any chance —"

Clover cuts her off. "No. Too much water under the bridge. You made your choice a long time ago. We've both moved on since then. Let's just forget about it, all right?"

Cliona nods a little sadly and walks back into the *Tatler* office.

When she's disappeared inside, Clover looks around. She then spots me — I'm still loitering beside the bike — and walks over to me, smiling.

"How are you feeling?" I ask.

She smiles. "Surprisingly good. I was dreading speaking to Cliona, but in the end it wasn't so bad. And let's be honest, Kendall's not a patch on Brains, is he? And what's with that weird Crombie accent?"

I smile and put on his voice: "I know. Mega out there, babes, yeah?"

She laughs. "Thanks for coming with me today. Knowing you were there, rooting for me, made all the difference."

"You're most welcome." I give her a hug. "Hey, I can't wait to read your new improved *Trinity Tatler*. Don't suppose you have room for a cub reporter?"

"Amy Green, hiring your own relations is highly irregular — nepotism, it's called. But . . . stranger things have happened." And then she gives me a mega-watt grin and a big wink. Clover Wildgust is back!

♥ Chapter 22

"Explain again why I have to be Miranda?" Clover moans. "'Cause I really wanted to be Samantha, and I'm not a happy camper in this suit. Where did you find it anyway? It's hideous." She hitches up the orange tweed skirt—even though she's doctored it with safety pins, it keeps sniggling down her hips.

I smile. "It used to be Sue's, from her school secretary days. She said I was welcome to it—it hasn't fit her in ten years."

"But it's still in her wardrobe?" Clover whistles. "She needs a serious spring cleaning." She glances at her watch. "What time do you have?"

"Twelve ten."

"Everyone's late."

What with all the Bailey drama-rama, I'd almost forgotten about Mum's bachelorette party. But here I am standing in front of the wooden gazebo in Saint Stephen's Green Park in Dublin's city center beside a very impatient Clover. I can't wait to see Mum's face when she realizes how much effort we've all put in.

"Where are they?" Clover mutters. "Come on, Monique."

On the other side of the gazebo, Russ, one of Dave's musician friends, is perched on a fold-up stool, guitar on his knee. (Russ and Dave used to be in a band together — the Colts, they were called — and today Russ is providing our background music.)

"Russ, could you play something calming to soothe Clover's twanging nerves?" I ask.

"Sure thing," he says, his eyes kind. I can't stop staring at them — they're dark hazel: the color of leaves turning in autumn. If it wasn't for his big woolly beard, he'd be quite cute for an old. He starts to strum on his guitar, and gentle, silky music ripples from his fingers and floats around our pop-up restaurant. Clover sits down at the table and rests her palms on the perfect linen tablecloth. (It's so stiff and crisp with starch that it crackled when the waiter Monique hired shook it out earlier.) She closes her eyes and takes a deep breath. *"Pooey,"* she says, opening her eyes again. "That pond stinks. Hope the scented candles start kicking in soon."

She's right — there is something damp and rotten lingering in the air. After lighting another of the posh orange-blossom candles, I take a second to admire our handiwork. Our cardboard sign, hand-painted with the words "THE BOATHOUSE," is hanging over the entrance to the gazebo. Two bay trees stand in pots, as though guarding the entrance; their trunks are decorated with red-ribbon bows, making them look like birthday presents. There are tea lights hanging in special jars from the white-planked roof, and huge scented candles stand in each corner. And, finally, the *pièce de résistance*, the perfectly laid table, complete with five golden chairs, each with a plush red-velvet seat, sparkling cutlery that you can see your face in, and three twinkling glasses at each setting.

In the center of each plate is a gold necklace. Not real gold — that would have cost a fortune — but gold-plated. Four of the necklaces have a single curling initial hanging from the chain: "M" for Miranda, "S" for Samantha, "B" for Big, and "C" for Charlotte. The fifth is an exact replica of Carrie's original necklace from the show. (Clover found it on the Internet.) That one is for Mum. It's her party, so she gets to play Ms. Bradshaw herself. We haven't told her a thing about

♥ 216

what we've got planned. Her "Carrie" costume — a white dress with an oversize silk flower corsage on one shoulder and a pair of Clover's high-heeled sandals — is sitting in a bag awaiting her arrival.

I sigh proudly and adjust the prissy cream "Charlotte" twinset I borrowed from Mills.

It wasn't easy putting the party together — Saffy had to apply for a special event's license to allow us to set up a "fashion shoot" in Saint Stephen's Green Park. Monique then begged her friend who runs a catering company to deliver the table and chairs, organize the food, and find us a waiter for the afternoon. It all came together in the end, though, with Clover and I coming up with the finishing touches — the red petals to scatter over the table, the tea lights, the scented candles, and the necklaces. (Even Dave helped by asking Russ to provide the live music.) Now the scene is set — the food is sitting in three large coolers, waiting to be served. All we need is Mum.

Suddenly Russ starts playing "Here Comes the Bride." Clover squeals and runs toward the doorway. I follow her.

Monique is walking across the park, leading Mum by the arm. Monique's wearing a black tuxedo, complete with a black bow tie. Her hair is slicked back with gel, she has "stubble" above her lip and on her chin, and her stuck-on eyebrows are thick and furry, like two black caterpillars.

Clover grins as they join us in the gazebo. "So good of you to join us, Mr. Big. And I see you've blindfolded your lady friend as requested. Nice job."

Monique bows. "I aim to please. And you're looking good, as always. Dig the suit."

"Can I take this off now?" Mum paws at the silk scarf tied across her eyes.

"Not for a minute," Clover says. "We're still waiting for Samantha. I think I see her coming, though."

"Who?" Mum asks, confused.

Someone's tottering toward us in red sandals with six-inch heels and a beige raincoat. As she draws nearer she unbuttons the coat, hangs it neatly over her arm, and lifts her sunglasses. It's Prue, dressed as Samantha.

She tinkles her fingers at us. "Darlings, so sorry I'm late. Traffic. And I'm not used to heels. Rather difficult to walk in, aren't they?" She wriggles her dress down her legs and then stands up straight. She purses her lips, and even dressed to kill in a hot red body-conscious dress that is so tight it looks as though glossy paint has been poured over her, she still looks like an uppity teacher.

We all stare at her, and Clover's mouth is open so

wide she looks like a pelican trawling for fish. "Well, *póggity póg*, Prue," she says. "Who'd have thought? Mrs. Stickleback—where have you been hiding those chili-hot curves? Hubba, hubba."

"I feel as though I'm wearing a swimsuit," Prue says, sounding flustered. "Are you sure it's not too much?"

"Not at all," Monique says. "If I was blessed with those curves, I'd flaunt them too. I'm Monique, by the way—aka Big." Monique sticks out her hand politely.

Prue shakes it. "Prue Stickleback. Um, Samantha, I suppose."

"Prue's Samantha?" Mum gasps. "And Monique's Big. I've got it! This is a *Sex and the City* party, isn't it, girls? Come on, you have to let me peek now."

Monique whips off Mum's blindfold and spreads her arms out theatrically. "Ta-da! Welcome to the Boathouse restaurant, baby," she says in a growly "Mr. Big" voice. "For your very own *Sex and the City* lunch. It's not Central Park—but it does have its very own lake and ducks. And Clover and Amy have a special 'Carrie' dress ready and waiting for you."

Mum squeals with delight. "Unbelievable! You girls never cease to amaze me. It's perfect. I'm speechless."

As her eyes sweep over the gazebo, her hand pressed over her mouth, she notices Russ and waves at him. "Taking requests, Russ?"

"Surely am, Sylvie. Let me guess? ABBA?"

Mum bites her lip. "Would you mind horribly?"

He smiles. "Not at all. Dave did warn me. I can even throw in a bit of Take That during dessert if you like." (Mum has such sad taste in music.)

"Oh, I like, I like." Mum's eyes glitter with happiness. I smile — so far, the party is going swimmingly.

♥ *Chapter 23*

I'm having a long sleep-in the next day when Mum comes into my room.

"You awake, Amy? Mills is on the phone. Talk to her, please. Otherwise I'll have to, and she's far too cheery for this hour of the morning."

"Mum, it's nearly lunchtime."

"I know, but Clover and Monique kept me up chatting nearly all night. I didn't get to bed till four. You were right to sneak off early." Last night we'd all shared Chinese takeout in front of the movie *When Harry Met Sally*, which is one of Mum's favorites. It was Dave's idea — he said lying on the sofa would be the perfect end to Sylvie's bachelorette party. He was right. Mum was thrilled.

After lunch in the park, we'd booked Mum an exclusive styling session in Brown Thomas, a fancy department store on Grafton Street. The rest of us had watched for hours as the stylist picked out loads of fabulously expensive clothes for Mum to try on in a special private room. They'd even provided champagne and smoked salmon. We felt like movie stars!

Mum fell in love with this beautiful dark-pink swishy dress, and Monique secretly bought it for her as an early wedding present. You should have seen Mum's face when Monique handed over the bag outside the shop. "I can't accept this, Monique," she'd squealed. "It's too much." Monique had shrugged and given one of her very French *pah*s. "You are my best friend, Sylvie. And I love you. Take it, please. Otherwise you will get a bread maker or toaster or something equally boring."

So Mum had kept the dress.

I take the phone off her and say, "Mills, can I call you back? I've just woken up."

"OK," she says. "I guess the party was a success, then?"

"Fantastic."

"Bailey says hi, by the way."

"How is he?"

"Good. We're going to the beach this morning. He's teaching me how to surf."

"Surf?" I try to picture Mills on a surfboard: crouched down, arms outstretched, waves splashing over her, hair flying in the wind . . . Nope, just can't see it.

"Are you laughing at me, Ames?" she asks crossly.

"Course not. But you do know saltwater ruins your hair?"

"It's in a French braid."

It's no use. I have to giggle.

"You *are* laughing at me."

"Not at all. You'll make a perfect surf chick. Bye, Mills. Oh, and tell Bailey I said hi back."

Mum smiles as she sits down on my bed. "I can't imagine Mills surfing."

I'm so used to her eavesdropping on my conversations that I don't even comment on it. "I know," I say instead. "But it's nice of Bailey to offer to teach her — he has his work cut out."

"How's Bailey dealing with being back at school? I haven't had a chance to ask you yet."

I shrug. "He seems to be coping all right. He only came back on Thursday, and all the teachers are being pretty decent to him. Especially Loopy — sorry,

223 ♥

Miss Lupin. She said that if he ever wanted to talk to someone, she was always available."

"Is she tallish with red hair and a rather odd dress sense?"

I smile. "That's her."

"I talked to her at a parent-teacher meeting once. She seemed nice."

"And Mills persuaded him to do the J Factor," I add. "So people will get to see how talented he is."

"What's the J Factor?"

"School singing competition — like the *X Factor*. Bailey's going to sing one of his own songs, and we're all going to cheer him on. You can come too if you like — and Dave."

"Thanks, Amy, that sounds fun. I'm glad he's OK. He's been through an awful lot in his life already." She pauses and sucks her teeth. "I told Finn what happened on the beach and about Bailey being in the hospital and everything. I hope you don't mind."

"Mum! You're always telling *me* not to interfere."

"I know, but this is different. Finn was so upset listening to it all, Amy. He excused himself and went and had a little cry in the backyard, I think. When he came back inside, his eyes were all red. If they'd just talk to each other . . . communicate in some way . . ." She breaks off and sighs. "Men can be so stubborn."

I remember what Mac said about how hard Bailey has always found it to communicate — that his true feelings only come out when he's singing — and then I have an idea. "Mum," I say slowly, "what do you think about inviting Finn to the J Factor?"

She stares at me for a long time before answering. "Are you sure it's not going to make things worse, Amy?"

"To be honest, I don't know. But I think Bailey's in a different place now. At least, I hope he is."

Mum squeezes my hand. "Then it's worth the risk. You're always determined to help people, no matter what, aren't you? You just bulldoze right in there, pushing everything else out of the way." She tries to put on my voice. "'No, stop, don't run away. I'm trying to help you.'"

I stare at her. "Mum, sometimes you may think you're complimenting me, but you're really not."

"I'm sorry. I guess your dogged enthusiasm just gets to me sometimes. I don't find life as easy as you seem to, and maybe I get a little jealous. And I'm a bit stressed out with all this wedding stuff. There's so much to do! Clover and Monique are being amazing, but Dave's not the most organized of people."

I roll my eyes. "He's a man, Mum. What do you expect?"

"Amy! You're far too young to be saying things like that."

I smile back at her. "Anyway, stop worrying, it'll all be fine. At the end of the day, a wedding's just a big party, and you like parties."

"You're right, Amy. I love parties. And sorry for having a moan at you."

I nudge her with my shoulder. "That's OK, Mum. I'm used to you and your moody blues by now."

"Hey!"

"Only kidding. I love you really."

"And I love you too, Amy. My special girl, all grown up." She brushes my hair back off my face and kisses me on the cheek.

"Mum! Stop being so soppy."

But you know something? I don't really mind. Sometimes Mum's not so bad.

♥ Chapter 24

The hours seem to creep by on Halloween, J Factor day. We've been off school all week (it's half-term, yeah!), and I'm delighted to report that the old gang—me, Seth, Mills, and Bailey—is back with a vengeance, although Mills and Bailey have spent most of the holiday wrapped around each other, playing tonsil hockey. But since they're both so happy, Seth and I don't really mind. And yes, we've had the odd lip-smacking session too. Rude not to join in, don't you think? We even did a test to see whose hearts were racing the hardest and fastest after a smooching session by taking each couple's pulses. Bailey and Mills, aka Romeo and Juliet, won, of course—boo! Although they have had a lot of practice this week.

It's nine o'clock now, and we're midway through the *J* Factor. I'm standing in the Saint John's hall, checking my watch nervously. The second half of the show's supposed to kick off any minute, but there's no sign of Mum yet.

Her plan was to arrive with Finn during the intermission — Bailey's not on until the second half, and Mum thought it would be better for Finn to slip in just as the lights were going down to avoid any sort of "fan" kerfuffle. Mum's got a lot of smarts sometimes — even Clover couldn't have come up with a better idea.

Clover really wanted to be here tonight, but Brains has whisked her off for a romantic weekend on the Aran Islands. They've gone to some diddly-eye traditional music and seafood festival, just the two of them. Since dealing with the Cliona conundrum, she's been in fantastic form. She only has one slight concern now: Amber Horsefell. "I think I'm starting to like her," Clover reluctantly admitted last night. "I caught myself laughing like a drain at one of her jokes today. *Très* worrying, Beanie. I can't be friends with a D4. It's against my religion."

I check my watch again. I'm really on edge. Mum and Finn have to get here soon — they just have to. I'm so nervous it was hard to concentrate on the first half of the show, and I know Mills and Seth felt the same. Dave and Mac clapped enthusiastically after every song, even after Annabelle Hamilton's warbling rendition of "Defying Gravity" from *Wicked*, complete with window-shattering top notes. But then they don't know what's to come. We haven't told either of them that Finn is coming.

"Wow, that girl has some pipes," Dave said as Annabelle took her third bow. The D4s in the seats behind us were going wild, cheering and whistling like they were at a rugby match. Annabelle has clearly been "applause training" them all week.

Out in the lobby, I try ringing Mum again, but she's still not answering.

Come on, I say under my breath. *Please!*

And then finally a text arrives: JUST PARKING THE CAR.

I almost pass out with relief when a minute later she rushes through the door, Finn at her heels. His eyes are flickering around nervously. He nods at me. "Hey, Amy."

"Hi, Finn." I smile back gently.

"Have we missed Bailey?" Mum puffs, her face flushed. "It took ages to find a space. I dumped the car on double yellow lines in the end—" She's cut off by a yell from our left.

"OMG, it's Finn Hunter from the telly!" Nina is squealing. The D4s with her all give high-pitched shrieks, like a chorus of fighting cats.

Finn gives them a wave — which makes them scream even louder.

"Take your seats, please, girls." Miss Lupin appears from inside the school hall, clipboard in hand. "The second half's about to commence."

"But, miss, it's Finn Hunter," Nina says. "Can we go and tell Annabelle? Maybe he'd put her on the telly."

"I'm not sure that's how it works, Nina," Loopy says patiently.

"Can I just say hi to him, then, miss, please?" she begs. "I'm his number-one fan!"

Loopy rolls her eyes. "If you must. But for goodness' sake, hurry up."

Nina immediately runs over and begins batting her ridiculously long fake eyelashes at Finn. "Can you autograph me?" She giggles manically and rolls her shirt up her arm.

"I don't do skin or clothes," Finn says. "Sorry, I'm just here to catch the show."

"Leave the poor man alone," Loopy says, shooing Nina toward the door with the clipboard. "Come along now, move."

"You all right, Finn?" Mum asks him in a low voice.

He nods silently — but he doesn't look great. The left side of his face is distorted. He must be chewing the inside of his cheek, just like Bailey does.

It's dark inside the hall, and Finn looks around, a little lost.

"We've kept a seat for you," I tell him. "Beside Mac."

"Mac?" he says anxiously. "You didn't tell me he'd be here, Sylvie."

Mum pats his arm. "You're both here for Bailey, remember that."

And before he has a chance to say anything else, the blue velvet stage curtain sweeps open to reveal a band of senior boys calling themselves Barcelona. They start blasting out a passable cover of "Mr. Brightside," an old Killers song.

We find our seats quickly, engineering it so that Finn and Mac are sitting beside each other. Mac stares at Finn as if he were a ghost. I was expecting him to be angry, but even in the gloom, I can see his eyes are sparkling with tears. He rubs his jaw, then stands up and pulls Finn into a rather awkward-looking hug and pats his back. They stay that way for a few seconds before pulling away and sitting down. I realize at that moment that Finn didn't just abandon Lane and Bailey — he left Mac behind too.

"Good to see you, lad," I hear Mac say over the music.

"I'm so sorry," Finn says. "I've made such a mess of everything."

"We both have." Mac pats Finn's hand. "We'll talk later. Let's listen to our boy sing, eh?"

Finn just nods.

After the band, one of the Crombies from our year, Hugo Hoffman, sings "Rehab" — which, I hate to admit, is surprisingly good. Next up are some transition-year D4s, who jiggle and shimmy around the stage in red Lycra dresses and heels to a Girls Aloud song. Only one of them, Candy Hutnell, has any talent, but they get a huge cheer from their cronies regardless.

And then finally, Bailey walks slowly onto the stage without making eye contact with the audience. We all clap and whoop: "Go, Bailey!"

He doesn't look up but settles himself on the stool, resting his guitar on his knee and staring at the floor.

Finn is gazing up at him, a hand over his mouth, and even from three seats away I can hear him taking loud, gulping breaths.

I nudge Seth. "Finn's as terrified as Bailey."

"Has Bailey seen him yet?" Mills asks.

"Don't think so," Seth says. "Hang on, wait a second . . ."

As if on cue, Bailey lifts his head, and his eyes sweep the first few rows of the audience. They stop on Mac . . . and Finn. His eyes rest on his dad's face. From the sudden rapid rise and fall of his chest, I'd say he's in shock. He had no idea that Finn was going to be here. We hadn't wanted to say anything in case Finn changed his mind, or in case knowing that his dad was coming would put Bailey off his performance. It was a risky decision, but we had agreed that it was the only way. I know we are all praying now that Bailey will sing so that Finn can see what an amazingly talented son he has. After that, none of us can predict what will happen. The rest is up to Bailey.

Bailey's gaze shifts from Finn to his grandpa: his family. I think having them both here supporting him, along with all his friends, is almost too much for him. Every one of us is smiling up at him eagerly, willing him on. He tears his eyes away from us and stares at the floor of the stage again.

Seth shakes his head. "This isn't looking good. Bailey had better start playing soon. The crowd's getting restless."

A whole minute later, Bailey still hasn't played a note. A low murmur is running across the hall, and one of the D4s has started to giggle. "Get on with it," a girl shouts from behind us. It sounds suspiciously like Nina's voice.

"Shush!" Mills says loudly, swinging round. "Give him a chance."

But Bailey is still just sitting there, head down, his left hand gripping the guitar fret so hard his fingers are white.

"*Siúcra*," I whisper. "We have to do something."

"Get him off the stage?" Seth suggests.

"No, make him sing," Mills says.

"But how?" I ask.

Mills shakes her head. "No idea. But we can't just leave him up there alone. He's dying."

"I could accompany him," Dave says. "What's he singing?"

"It's one of his own," Mac pipes up. "So it's a kind thought, but you won't know it, mate. I know someone who might, though. Finn, the song he's doing, it's one of Lane's old ones, 'Atlantic Blues.' He's set new words to it. Do you remember the melody?" Finn nods and Mac pats his hand. "He needs you, lad. Get up there. Just do your best."

After a few long seconds, Finn finally stands up.

As he climbs onto the stage, the whole hall erupts with shouts and whistles, and several of the D4s pretend to swoon. Finn and Bailey stare at each other, and then Finn sits down at the piano to the left of the stage, stretches his hands out, and starts to play strong, haunting music, his fingers tripping lightly over the keys.

"Finn's pretty good," Seth says. "Did you know he could play, Amy?"

"I had no idea." Then: "Come on, Bailey," I whisper under my breath. "Play!"

Agonizingly slowly, Bailey starts to strum his guitar.

"Thank God," Mum says, her hand fluttering to her chest. "I don't think my heart can take much more."

Finn continues to play, and slowly Bailey opens his mouth. *"You abandoned me once,"* he sings, his distinctive, husky voice soaring, making the whole hall immediately hush. *"You were young and scared. Then I called to you twice, there was no one there."* The song sounds familiar yet brand-new, like all good songs, and Bailey is rocking it, his face screwed up in concentration.

"I called in the dark, I begged for my mother. I cried and I cried, but no one delivered." He takes a deep breath and continues: *"So I hate you, hate you, hate you, and*

all you do. For leaving, leaving. My soul beaten black and blue. Abandoned, yeah, yeah, yeah, Abandoned."

I look at Mum. She's sniffing and tears are streaming down her face. (She's such a softie.) Mills is crying too, and Mum passes her a tissue. I'm on the verge of it myself — the lyrics are pretty powerful.

Bailey strums heavily, picking up the tempo, while Finn plays on in the background, his face set rigid. He looks stern, but I think he's trying not to break down.

Bailey gets to his feet then and swings his guitar around: lost in the music. The cheers and claps are so loud, they nearly take the roof off.

Bailey's last chord is lost in the eruption of applause. And then a miraculous thing happens — Finn hugs Bailey, and Bailey hugs him back. It's awkward — there's a guitar in the way for a start — but it's a hug, and that's a very good beginning. When they pull away, Finn holds Bailey's hand in the air and makes him take a bow.

Dave smiles at Mum and wipes her tears away with his fingers. Meanwhile, Mac is sobbing so hard he can barely breathe, and Mills is staring up at Bailey, beaming through her tears and clapping wildly. "Bailey!" she shouts. "You did it!"

He looks down at her, smiles, and blows her a kiss. Pure joy lights up her face, and I'm so happy for her and Bailey. But most especially for Bailey. I jump to my feet, cheering and whooping. I'm quickly followed by Seth, Mills, Mum, Dave, and Mac. Soon everyone is giving Bailey a standing ovation—the applause is deafening.

"Talk about star quality!" I yell at Seth.

"And look at his face. He's ecstatic."

Seth's right. Bailey's beaming from ear to ear, lapping up all the applause, his fist lifted in the air like a champion. Finn is right by his side, holding his other hand aloft too.

"I think they're going to be OK," I say. "Finn and Bailey."

"Thanks to you," Seth says. "You never gave up on Bailey, not once. You really are something, Amy Green."

And with that he kisses me on the cheek, making my own heart soar.

Acknowledgments

This book would not have been possible without a *lot* of people's help. First up my family: Mum, Dad, Kate, Emma, and Richard. OK, Richard didn't really help at all (little brothers, you know how it is!), and Kate is working in New Zealand, so technically they weren't of any practical use, but they're still family and I still love them to bits! Ben, Sam, Amy, and Jago were, however, very much on hand. Ben never complains when I take off to festivals or on tours; Sam is always a mine of information on all things teen, whether he knows it or not; and Amy and Jago entertain me on a daily basis with their various shenanigans.

As always, I have to thank my dear friends Andrew, Tanya Delargy, and Nicky "Pleasantly Decorated" Cullen (see, I put your second names in this time, those that wanted me to—I do listen!). In every book I have to rotate the order of the names so no one gets jealous. Honestly, you'd think my friends were three years old sometimes.

And of course huge kudos to my writer friends, fellow travelers on the book path, especially the fab and lovely Martina Devlin, who makes me think—which is always a good thing. Judi Curtin is always cheerful and a rock of good sense, and David Maybury makes me laugh on a weekly basis, for which he deserves a Giggler's Medal.

I thank my agents, Philippa Milnes-Smith and Peta Nightingale, for their good counsel and unerring enthusiasm, and the gang in Children's Books Ireland (CBI) for flying the kiddie-lit flag in Ireland. Tom is off to pastures new, and I wish him all the best in his quest.

I salute the gals and girls of Walkerville for being such Amy cheerleaders. I continue to have a ball working with all of you. My editors, Gill Evans and Annalie Grainger, deserve huge thanks for pouring the book into its best party dress; the lovely Jo Hump-D, Jane Harris, Eve, Ruth, and Alice supplied the party invitations, streamers, and hooters; Sean, Hanna, Heidi, and the gang were certainly at the party; and Katie was in charge of hair and makeup, and a lovely job she did too. And Conor Hackett continues to be the Irish party coordinator and general ringmaster supreme. And a huge thanks to Sarah and Nicola for the beautiful new covers.

I must mention my special teen editor and fount of all knowledge, Kate Gordon. Kate has been part of the Amy team right from the start. And I look forward to recruiting several more clever and smart young editors very soon. And a big shout-out to fellow book fan Michelle in Navan, and hi to Ella Tubs, just 'cause you asked so nicely, Ella!

Can't forget the children's booksellers near and far, who have been so good to me over the years, especially Superhero of the Children's Book World, David O'Callaghan, for all his support and the fab mixtapes; the fantastic Dubray gang, especially Susan, Ruth, Kim, and Mary Esther; and the lovely Mary Bridget in Hodges Figgis.

To Erin Carolan, winner of the Ask Amy Green Facebook competition, and last but certainly not least, you, the uber-cool reader. For all your e-mails, letters, cards, and photos, I thank you. It's YOU that makes writing worthwhile. I thank you, Amy thanks you, Clover thanks you . . .

Please do drop me a line. I love hearing from Amy Greensters. My e-mail is sarah@askamygreen.com. Or check out the Ask Amy Green fan page on Facebook.

Best,
Sarah XXX

Mills's ballerina sister has just landed the role of a lifetime — but something is very wrong with the young dancer. A worried Mills asks best friend Amy for help. How can Amy refuse, even though she has Big Problems of her own to solve?

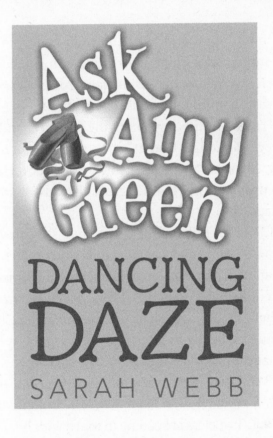

Turn the page for an excerpt . . .

♥

I'm in my best friend Mills's ultratidy bedroom when her mum, Sue, walks in, a huge grin on her face. "There's someone here who wants to speak to you," she says, handing the house phone to Mills.

"Hello?" Mills says into the receiver, and then her eyes light up. "Claire!" she squeals. "You haven't rung for ages and ages. How's your toe? Has the nail dropped off yet? Is there still loads of snow in Budapest?"

Claire is Mills's big sister, and she moved to Budapest when she was fifteen to study ballet at the Budapest Ballet Academy. She's now a soloist, and the company is dancing *Romeo and Juliet* in a big theater in Dublin just before Christmas, and Claire is playing Juliet! Dad's bank is sponsoring the event, so he's already booked us all tickets to see her.

"When will you be home for *Romeo and Juliet*?" Mills is asking now. (Claire may be a brilliant dancer, but she's hopeless at keeping in touch with her family, and I know Mills misses her horribly.)

♥ An excerpt from *Ask Amy Green: Dancing Daze*

Mills's eyes widen. "Holy Moly!" she shrieks, bouncing up and down on the bed with excitement. "That's brilliant news. And I can't believe you'll be on the telly." There's a pause. "Oh, OK. I'll tell Mum. Love you too!" Mills clicks the phone off and hands it back to Sue. "Claire said to say bye and that she'll e-mail you her flight details. Did you know about the publicity trip, Mum?"

Sue shakes her head. "I had no idea. Isn't it brilliant? I can't wait to see her. Now, Amy looks like she's about to explode with curiosity, so I'll leave you to tell her the news." She leans over and gives Mills a hug. "My two girls, back under the same roof." Her eyes water and she waves a hand in front of her face. "Sorry, I just miss her so much."

"Me too, Mum," Mills says.

Sue was right. I am dying to know the news, so as soon as she's out the door, I turn to Mills. "What's happening? Sounds pretty exciting."

"Claire's coming home next Thursday to do some preshow publicity for *Romeo and Juliet*. She'll be here for only a couple of days, but she's going to be on the *Late Late Show* on Friday night with the Hungarian dancer who plays Romeo. She wants us to come to the airport to collect her. You too, if you like."

"No way!" I say. "That's fantastic. All the olds

An excerpt from *Ask Amy Green: Dancing Daze* ♥

in Ireland watch that show. She's going to be mega-famous after it. And yes, please. I do love a good airport reunion. Count me in."

On the way to Dublin airport the following Thursday evening, Mills and I take one final look at *Ballet Barbie*, the book I helped Mills create for her sister. Mills wanted to make a special scrapbook to celebrate Claire's homecoming, and with my aunt Clover's assistance, I found this amazing website called makeabook.com. Clover knows everything about everything, and at eighteen, with her long white-blond hair, rock-star boyfriend, and job at the *Goss* teen magazine, she's the coolest aunt around.

The makeabook site allows you to pick a style, then scan in photos (and anything else you'd like to see on the pages), add text, and preview it carefully (checking for any spelling mistakes). You press "print"—and *voilà*: two days later, a rather fabulous one-of-a-kind book arrives in the post. (Clover very sweetly paid for the book on her credit card and refused to let Mills pay her back.)

Mills carefully opens the ballet-shoe-pink hardcover. "'To Ballet Barbie, Lots and lots of love, Mills,'" she reads. "Ballet Barbie" is Mills's nickname for her big sis.

♥ An excerpt from *Ask Amy Green: Dancing Daze*

"'Chapter One,'" she continues. "'The Early Days. From the very beginning, Claire Starr was born to dance. Her mum, Sue, says Claire was bopping along to the radio as soon as she could stand. As a tiny tot, Claire especially loved dancing to the Spice Girls.'"

Sue laughs from the front passenger seat. "She certainly did. I used to call her 'Dancing Spice.'"

"That's true," Mills's dad agrees quietly. I like Allan Starr, but he is very, very normal. Some people may even call him boring. . . . I've only ever seen him in a checked shirt and beige chinos. Clover says the most exciting thing about him is the unusual spelling of his name.

Mills points to one of the photos in chapter one, an adorable image of Claire as a little girl wearing a tiny white tutu, both hands over her head, fingers touching, like a real ballerina.

"Already performing at three," Mills says.

I smile. "That's such a cute shot."

"She started at Miss Smitten's School of Dance just after that," Sue says. "By the time she was five, she insisted on going to two classes a week. Remember, Allan?"

Allan laughs heartily and slaps the steering wheel. "Do I ever. When I told her it was too expensive, she said it could be her birthday present *and* her

An excerpt from *Ask Amy Green: Dancing Daze* ♥

Christmas present. I nearly fell off my chair. Imagine being that smart and determined at five!" He shakes his head. "But I guess all that determination has paid off."

We flick through the rest of the book: Claire, age six, dressed in rags as the Little Match Girl for one of her ballet school's shows; Claire, age eleven, doing an elegant arabesque in a plain pink cross-backed leotard.

We also added her ballet exam reports, all glowing, and some old cuttings from the Irish newspapers, including the front-page photograph of Claire in a full-length white tutu just after she'd been accepted at the Budapest Ballet Academy. Her dark brown eyes are staring proud and strong at the camera.

After we've studied the final page, an *Irish Times* piece about her upcoming starring role as Juliet in Dublin that calls her the "Irish Ballerina," Mills closes the book carefully and runs her hands over the front cover. "Do you think she'll like it?" she asks, biting her lower lip nervously.

"She'll adore it," I say. "I promise."

♥ An excerpt from *Ask Amy Green: Dancing Daze*